Jazz

Happily After When

A 12 book series, inspired by fairytales and the ugliness of real life.
Books are sequential, and highly recommended to be read in publication order.

Jazz
An Aladdin retelling

Aria
A Little Mermaid Retelling

Cara
A Cinderella Retelling

Sachi
A Snow White Retelling

And more to follow...

HAPPILY AFTER WHEN BOOK 1

when marriage means business

Jazz

EMILY BOURNE

First Published by Halo & Claws Publishing 2020

JAZZ

Happily After When - Book 1

For information contact: https://www.hcpbooks.com

Stock Images via Bigstock, Shutterstock

ISBN: 978-1-925990-05-8

What does happily ever after mean?

Does it exist?

Remember the victim.

Successor

"Jazz," Mr Yuki says, raising his wine glass. "Congratulations on completing your university studies one year early. Darius, you must be very proud. Not only an academic success; your daughter also runs the most successful gym in your empire."

Darius boasts a proud smile at the head of the long-stretched, oak dining table. "Indeed, Kourin. Jazz is an exceptional daughter."

Jazz sinks into her plush dining chair at the opposite end to her father. The smiling faces on either side of the table turn her way, raising their glasses in a toast. She pinches her beige linen napkin and focuses on the flickering light of the tall centrepiece candles.

"Our Caden could have graduated early, too," Mrs Walsh says zealously, wrapping her arm around her son's. "But he's there to learn as much as he can. Isn't that right, Caden?"

"Yes, Mother," Caden says, a twitch to his lips wanting to mock his mother's devotion to him.

Jazz takes a small sip of red wine, aware this is a night to remember. The Yuki, Walsh, and Roth families sit in celebration of her.

Knowing the ins and outs of these wealthy families, Jazz is mindful of motives to this dinner, which have nothing to do with her. Even the mayor of Maiden City is here to butter up her father.

Sachi Yuki beams a cheery grin towards Jazz, and asks, "What do you plan to do now that you're finished with university? Still run the gym?"

Jazz combs her fingers through her lush, raven hair, pushing it over her shoulder. "I'm studying for my masters." She eyes the head of the table and smiles at her father. "Whilst moving into senior management."

Darius grins and turns to Mayor Walsh. "My daughter has big dreams."

Jazz's fingers flex and her knuckles crack as her father smiles at Mayor Walsh's laughter. *My management is laughable?*

"Ethan," Mayor Walsh says, swishing his wine glass. "How did you go with the numbers I sent you?"

Ethan grins and nods to the Mayor. "Perfectly. Thank you, again."

"Good, good. They always serve me well, especially in cleaning up this city," Mayor Walsh slurs over his wine glass. "The crime coming out of The Limits is infecting all of Maiden City."

"Are you still thinking of shutting that area down?" Mr Yuki asks.

"Someone has to do something about it," Mayor Walsh says. "And seems I'm the man with that title."

Caden Walsh groans and sits back in his chair. "Why don't you just move the city limits, and then those people will officially not be your problem?"

"That's one way to lose a lot of land, young man," Mr Roth says with a mocking grin.

Caden smirks. "*Whatever.*"

"Enough business," Mrs Walsh interjects.

"Here, here," Mr Roth says. "None of that at the table."

"Certainly," Mayor Walsh says. "Darius, how's the old ticker?"

Darius straightens his tie. "You know doctors, they like to load you up on pills."

"So you're doing ok?" Mrs Yuki asks, squeezing the hand of her daughter Sachi.

Jazz's breathing falters as frown lines pull at her father's face.

Darius brightens, looking kindly on Mrs Yuki. "I'm doing well, but it has come to the time that naming a successor is increasingly necessary."

When her father came to this country from Persia, he had nothing to his name. His name meant nothing. He met David Roth at temple before either married. They encouraged each other to grow their businesses and were great companions. Jazz often wonders if Ethan sought her father's mentorship because his business did the best out of the pair. Not that David Roth did poorly. The Roth Manor is two streets away from the Abadi Mansion in the prestigious area of Sovereign Hill.

Caden turns to Jazz, his eyebrows raised in interest. "Up for it?" he asks her.

Jazz is one to keep her cards close to her chest. Her eyes wander to Ethan. Her father's mentee and her number one competition. She breathed a little easier when Ethan took over his father's company last year. But Ethan is someone you can't turn your back on.

"Eve," Mrs Walsh says to Mrs Roth opposite her. "I hear you and David are going on another voyage."

Mayor Walsh takes a large sip of wine, and adds, "Retirement treating you well, I see."

"We can't get enough of island-hopping," Mrs Roth giggles, eyeing her husband.

David Roth smiles and nods. "It was the best timing for Ethan to take the reins at the company."

Ethan stares at his dinner plate, nostrils flaring to suppress his disdain.

Jazz stares at the tension bulging in his eyes and tries to

understand him. Ethan has everything she could ever want. He has control of his father's company. His parents aren't watching over every move he makes. They are jumping from one vacation to the next. Jazz has worked her entire life to get to where Ethan is. When she played with dolls as a child, she wasn't homemaking; she was running a board of directors. The annoyance radiating off Ethan infuriates her.

Caden swipes his father's wine glass while he's distracted and slurps it back. He places the glass to its original position and shakes his head at Jazz.

"Jazz," Sachi pipes up. "Can we go outside?"

Caden stands up, tossing his linen napkin on the table. "I'll escort these ladies outside."

Jazz stands and nods at her father. "Father, I trust it's ok you excuse us from the table?"

Darius waves a hand. "Of course, my dear."

As Caden and Sachi stand with her, Jazz eyes Ethan and asks, "Coming?"

Ethan smirks. "No. You kids have fun."

Jazz frowns and controls her eyes not to roll. She and Caden are twenty, and Sachi is still in high school, so twenty-eight-year-old Ethan likes to act superior to them. *Age doesn't make you impressive*, Jazz concludes.

Jazz stretches out her arm, welcoming Sachi to walk beside her. She rubs Sachi's arm and they follow Caden through the lavish living area towards the ornately carved rear doors. They walk out to the marble-tiled pool decking, overlooking the infinity pool and immaculately landscaped gardens, illuminated by lighting hidden in the hedges.

As they take in the crisp night air and meander around the cushioned lounge seating, Jazz pulls out her phone and scrolls through her Collage feed. Thousands of hearts flood her notifications, and she ponders whether it's the right time to post a new image. *Maybe a*

Namaste yoga pose?

While her thumbs tap away, she glances at Caden and Sachi whispering together. Caden backs Sachi against a wall with his hand pressed by her face as he leans in with his trademark, charisma-oozing, smile.

Jazz watches Caden's other hand slide around Sachi's hip and pulls her closer to him.

"Caden," Jazz says, slipping her phone in her pocket and marching towards them. "Ever hear of personal space?"

Caden pulls himself upright and drops his hands beside him. "Lighten up, Abadi. We're just talking."

Jazz clasps Sachi's hand. "Talk with your mouth, not your hands."

"Whatever," Caden smirks.

"Hey, what was that remark between your father and Ethan?" Jazz asks him.

"What remark?" Caden asks.

"About numbers," Jazz elaborates.

Caden shrugs. "Probably another mess to clean up. There's always someone on Dad's list who'll fix something for a price." Caden's phone rings, and he pulls it from his trousers' pocket. He grins and shows the girls the screen. "Nice, it's Liz."

Jazz rolls her eyes and suppresses her gag. *Another one of his one-day romances.*

Caden lifts his phone to his ear and begins his charm act, walking away from the girls toward a chair to recline in.

Jazz squeezes Sachi's hand and meets her eyes. "Remember, you are in charge of your body. No one can touch you without your permission."

Sachi touches her cheek bashfully. The rose in her cheeks highlights against the porcelain of her skin. "It was nothing, Jazz."

"Nothing can turn into something. Be careful, Sachi. You're only sixteen, and people will try to take advantage of your vulnerability.

You need to be aware of your surroundings, and the people you let close."

Sachi giggles nervously. "You sound paranoid."

Jazz drops Sachi's hand and smiles. "Maybe I am."

Caden and Sachi return to their parents, ready to leave for the evening. Jazz peruses the dining table, and Ethan is missing. Her eyebrows raise as she notes her father's absence.

She moves towards her father's study, and an uneasy twinge cramps her stomach. She edges toward the closed double doors and holds a breath as she leans her ear in.

Footsteps sound from inside and she jumps backward with alarm. A handle turns, and one of the heavy mahogany doors pulls open. Her father walks Ethan out of his study, a hand placed on his back.

"Thank you, Darius," Ethan says, extending his hand.

"Pleasure," Darius says, shaking Ethan's hand.

Ethan nods at Jazz. "Evening."

"Goodbye," she says warily, as Ethan walks past her down the hall. She looks at her father with puzzlement. "You and Ethan had a meeting?"

Her father clears his throat. He beckons her into his study. "Let's talk."

Jazz straightens her back and calmly walks into the study.

"I'll see off our guests and be right back."

"Shouldn't I—" Jazz begins, but her father is already walking down the hall. She knows the Yukis and Walshs were already out the door, so she moves further into the study.

She sits on a high-backed leather armchair in front of her father's desk. *Why was he in a private meeting with Ethan?*

Her eyes wander over the packed bookcases behind the expansive desk; to all the biographies of the world's greatest thinkers, to the procedures her father built his business on. Her gaze lowers to the desktop, and a document folder steals her attention. Nothing exceptional about the folder except it lays askew on the desk. Her father would never leave something so out of place. It must be Ethan's.

She stands and moves around the desk. Her hand tremors as she reaches for the folder.

"Ok," her father says, clapping his hands together as he strides into the study.

She jumps away from the desk, tucking her hands behind her back, and tries to shake the deer-in-headlights look.

"I have something I want to discuss... Jazz? Is something wrong?"

"No, nothing," she's quick to reply. She slips around the desk to the armchair. "What do you need to tell me?"

Darius lets out a weighted sigh. He sits behind his desk and sets his palms on the folder. "Ethan pulled me aside."

Jazz swallows uncomfortably, waiting for him to add more.

He lifts the folder. "This is his proposal to take over as CEO."

"No!" it rushes out of her, loud and frantic.

Darius lifts a hand. "Jazz, please compose yourself."

Jazz fixes her hair and settles in the chair. "Sorry, Father."

"I know you're working hard, studying to be my successor. You're an Abadi. I want you as the head of the company. However, Ethan is the front runner. He's already brought three big clients to the company. He's proven his worth." Darius wrings his hands and looks deep into Jazz's eyes. "The board doesn't have faith in you. You have a lot to prove."

"How can they not have faith in me?" Jazz rubs her chest as every word she speaks weighs her down.

"You're young and fresh out of university. I wish there was more time, but this is it," her father says, low and slow. "Prove yourself, Jazz. The board meeting is in a week."

Jazz stands and smooths her skirt. "Don't worry, Father. I will be your successor."

Proposal

Jazz arches her back as she reclines on a leg press machine the next day. She lifts her phone high and tilts her face for the perfect angle. *Snap.*

Jazz pulls herself up and scrolls through the photos she took this morning. She needs the perfect image to gain maximum engagement. Not only does she run the best Ultimate ME gym in a prime Business District location, she is also head of social media marketing for the company.

She bounces off the machine, and scrolls through the stats of her Collage account on the walk to her office. She slides onto her desk chair and puts her phone down. The stark white walls of her office soothe her as she wakes her computer. Her business plan appears on the screen. The CEOship is her birthright. Ethan will not swoop in and steal it from her.

She is the Abadi heiress.

Her phone buzzes from the table. She groans as the screen illuminates with *Ethan Calling*.

"Speak of the devil," Jazz says, lifting the phone. She hits answer. "Ethan. Hello."

"Such a warm greeting," Ethan replies with a hint of laughter to his words.

"I'm just busy running my company," she bites back. "What can I do for you?"

"I think you mean running your site. You're not CEO."

"Yet."

Ethan lets out a throaty laugh. "As much as I like a good dose of healthy competition, I was hoping we could work together on this. Care to meet me for dinner tonight?"

"Dinner?"

"Yes."

"What do you mean work together? There can only be one CEO." Jazz reclines on her chair and kicks her heels on the desk with a grin. "Unless you mean you want to help me become CEO?"

"Meet me for dinner. I'll explain everything to you over cocktails."

Drinks could make him talk too much and give me an advantage in the boardroom.

Jazz moves her feet off the desk and sits upright. She grabs a pen and sighs. "Ok, where am I meeting you?"

"Overity in the Night Club District."

Gross. "Ok, I can be there at eight."

"I'd prefer seven."

"I don't know about you, but I work for a living, so I can't be at your beck and call."

Ethan splutters a laugh. "How nicely passive aggressive of you, Jazz."

"I thought you'd appreciate me speaking in your first language."

"Keep that spirit for tonight. We have a lot to discuss." And with that, he leaves Jazz with beeping of a disconnected call.

She drops her phone, wincing. "Goodbye to you, too."

"Jazz," says Marcus, a personal trainer, knocking on the

doorframe of her office. "Can we talk for a minute?"

Jazz gestures to the chair opposite her desk. "The minute is all yours."

He smiles nervously, moving to the chair. "Well, I might need more than a minute."

She raises an eyebrow as he sits. "I don't like the body language, Marcus. You're not quitting, are you?"

Marcus slumps in the chair, exhaling a heavy breath. "I'm sorry. I've been offered this amazing opportunity to—"

"—No," Jazz cuts him off. "No way." She twirls her pen furiously. "What's the monetary offer? We will match it. We can't lose you."

Marcus folds his arms across his torso. "It's not about the money. There's no room to grow here."

"You're second in command. I can't promote you, or you'd have my position."

"I have your job whenever you're absent without notice," Marcus continues, a sharp edge to his words. "I take on the work, come in early, all without notice. But what's the reward?"

"You are aware you're speaking to the future CEO of this company?" Jazz drops the pen and calms her pace. "What are we not providing for you?"

"This site is the best in the company." His jaw flexes. "But you're such a control freak. Any time any of us try to expand or take on extra responsibility, you take it from us." He takes a large breath to continue on. "It's great to have a boss that is so committed and active in the gym, but you rob us the joy of the work."

Jazz's eyes widen, and her nostrils flare. A line of sweat drops to the left of her forehead. She stands and slams her hands on the desk. "Get out. You're finished here, effective immediately."

"Jazz, I didn't mean any disrespect," he says, quickly standing up. "I still like you and—"

"—Now!" she snaps, arm stretched, pointing to the door. "You're done at Ultimate ME. Don't you dare think about grovelling back here."

Marcus swiftly leaves her office and Jazz collapses in her chair. Her chest rapidly rises and falls. She fixes her hair and wipes her brow. *How dare he?*

She sits up straight and plants her trembling hands on the desk. *I am Jazz Abadi. No one talks to me like that. I will run this company.*

That evening, Jazz wraps an intricate Kashmiri hand-embroided pashmina shawl around her shoulders. She fixes the waves of her hair amongst the drapes of the shawl.

Flashes of light blind her vision as she walks from the taxi. She squints open her eyes to paparazzi snapping her picture. *Ugh, can't I go anywhere without someone recognising me?*

She hurries inside Overity.

"Jazz," Ethan says, throwing his arms wide and swivelling on his bar stool. "So glad you could join me." He stands from the stool and extends a hand. "Can I take your shawl?"

She lifts a hand. "I don't intend to stay long enough to warrant taking it off."

Ethan lets out a boisterous laugh which forces him to hold his stomach. Jazz holds her resolve, no matter how tempting it is to roll her eyes.

Ethan picks up his martini. "What can I get you?"

Jazz places her clutch on the bar and addresses the bartender. "I'll have a cosmopolitan and I'll be taking care of Mr Roth's tab."

"Now, now. There'll be none of that," Ethan says. "I asked you to dinner."

As the bartender starts on her drink, Jazz replies, "I don't think dinner is necessary. You can say what you need to say over one drink."

"One drink, hey?" Ethan smirks. "We'll see."

Jazz bites her tongue, reminding herself she came here to squeeze information out of Ethan, not to engage with him.

They move to a table and Ethan gestures to the dark romance of dim lighting, riardwood and aged leather. "Surely this would make a good background for your social media feed."

"It's a fitness page. Booze doesn't exactly fit the aesthetic."

Ethan places his glass on the table and relaxes into the baby-soft leather wing chair. "Your father told you about our meeting?"

"Of course he did. My father and I always discuss business."

"Even when it's not your business."

"Don't make this personal, Ethan."

"We've known each other a long time, which makes it personal."

The bartender hands Jazz her drink. She takes a sip, hoping it takes quick effect. "What is the point of this meeting?"

Ethan pulls a rolled up document from the inside pocket of his jacket. "My business plan involves you, Miss Abadi."

Jazz's eyes slit from his overly familiar pronunciation of her surname. Her fingers curl as she wills herself to wait for him to elaborate.

"Please," he says, gesturing to the document placed on the table. "Take a look."

"You're giving me your business plan when the board meeting is in less than a week? You want to lose?"

He tilts his head. "You think your only way of winning is by looking at my business plan?"

She relents and rolls her eyes. She swipes the document and flips it open. "Why are you showing me this?"

Ethan leans across the table and touches her knee. "Because I need you on my team."

Jazz's stomach flips, and she whacks his hand away. "Team?"

He pulls back and digs in the other pocket of his jacket. "Here's the pivotal part of my plan." He places a small box on the table. "The proposal."

Jazz swallows bile as she eyes the box. "The what?"

Ethan opens the box and a large princess cut diamond shines a top a platinum ring.

Jazz chugs her drink and lifts the empty glass, gaining the bartender's attention. "Another!"

"What do you say?" Ethan says like he's asking her to share a side plate.

"Are you seriously asking me to marry you?"

"You know I'm the front runner for CEO," he says, lacing his hands. "But your father whispered to the board that an Abadi should run the company. The decision between the right move and pleasing Darius has confused the board. Let's put them at ease. Marry me and bring me officially into the Abadi family. Run the company with me."

Jazz stands, her heart palpitating. "You're mad."

"You don't stand a chance, Jazz." He stands and wraps an arm around her low back. His fingers press into the fabric of her dress and she shivers like he's touching her bare flesh. "Work with me. Let's be a team and move Ultimate ME into the future."

"Are you suggesting co-CEOs?"

"No, of course not." His fingers explore downwards. "The board wants to name me CEO. We will give them what they want and you can help with decisions in the background."

Jazz grabs his hand and twists at his wrist. He yelps in pain. She tosses his hand away, and whispers harshly, "You want me to be some kind of doting housewife?"

Ethan shakes off his hand and smiles. "I'd love to see you in an apron."

The bartender comes by with Jazz's drink. Jazz throws it back and plants the empty glass on the tray before it's moved an inch. "Another."

"Thirsty?" Ethan jokes.

"Trying to block out your stupid voice."

Ethan nods to her empty seat. "Sit, please. Let's talk about this."

Jazz's head spins with the weight a feather. The effects of a swift vodka intake take her over. She sits out of necessity, pinching the bridge of her nose.

"Did you hear me?" Ethan's voice warbles into focus.

She drops her hand and finds his face. "Huh?"

"Do you want to go over the proposal with me?" He slides the document closer to her and sits the ring box behind it. "Our marriage would be the ultimate power move. We'd be unstoppable."

You mean you'd be unstoppable. Did I say that out loud or not?

Another cranberry-soaked vodka lands in front of her. She pulls it to her lips like a life-force.

"Are you just going to keep drinking instead of taking this seriously?"

Jazz slams the glass on the table. "Seriously? No, I won't take marrying you seriously."

Ethan straightens his tie and moves from his chair to her side. Before Jazz can react, his hands sneak under her shawl and massage her shoulders.

"If it's bothering you, we can get intimate to get you in the mood."

Jazz gags at the thought. She leans forward, moving the shawl over her head and hiding in the darkness. "Grotesque."

Ethan laughs. "You know, I am named one of Maiden City's hottest bachelors."

Jazz drapes the shawl around her face like a hood. "Maybe because you should be lit on fire."

"Either way," he says, rounding back to his chair, "you will lose. At least being with me you might have some say in what goes on."

Jazz snatches his half-empty martini and kicks it back. With her vision blurring, she makes a sloppy getaway to the front door.

"Hey, where are you going?" Ethan calls out. "I thought you were paying."

His laughter trails behind her as she escapes to the streets.

15

Guilt

Adrian hangs his throbbing head and fidgets with his ill-fitting suit as he walks inside the shelter. His gut pangs with guilt as he avoids the common room. His eyes run over the peeling paint, holes in the walls, the bowed ceiling above, and the torn vinyl flooring below. The mess of thoughts hurry his steps, and he jumps when someone grabs his arm.

"How'd it go?" Eddy asks. His green eyes shine with a mix of hope and apprehension.

Adrian twists his lips, heaves his chest, and falls into a sluggish stance.

Eddy spins him by the shoulders. "Come into my office."

Adrian lets Eddy push him easily, too exhausted to disagree.

"What happened?" Eddy asks, sitting on the edge of his desk. "I knew I should have gone with you."

Adrian flops on the couch and sighs, rubbing his temples. "No, you needed to be here... We had no one else to stay."

"You look haggard."

Adrian blows out a breath. "Thanks." He finds Eddy's eyes. "Six weeks."

Eddy brightens. "Six weeks and we get the money?"

Adrian's posture drops again as he shakes his head. "Six weeks until they decide yes or no."

"What?" Eddy gasps. "How can it take that long?"

Adrian shrugs. "That's government agencies for you."

"They didn't make you sign anything, did they?" Eddy asks, alarmed.

Adrian shakes his head. "No, I told you I wouldn't do that without you." He takes a slip of paper from his jacket and hands it to Eddy. "They gave me this. I told them to tell me what it said."

Eddy reads over the paper. "I've already seen this. This is fine." He jumps off the desk and says, "You need to go corporate."

"No. No way. I am not stooping that low."

"Adrian, we can't wait six weeks for *maybe* a yes."

"I know that." He pinches the bridge of his nose and winces. "I shouldn't have asked for a government grant."

"Why not? We're a not-for-profit. We're the people they want to help."

Adrian stands, face softening as he approaches Eddy. "We won't get it because of me. They'll check my background and dig up my past. I'll be the reason we don't get the money and the shelter will be shut down."

"Don't let the negative thoughts in," Eddy says, patting Adrian's shoulder. "Maybe they're more concerned with your age? Some people don't take nineteen-year-olds seriously."

"Yeah... Maybe."

"You want to get into this? We could have a session now?"

Adrian smiles, patting Eddy's hand. "Thanks, but no. I should get back out there."

"You're too stressed to—"

"—Bud, I'm fine. Don't worry about me. Just do the amazing work you do." He pulls the door open. "Work will be a good distraction for me.”

Adrian leaves Eddy’s office and takes the narrow hallway to the dining room. Hector and Maria have set up the food on a trestle table and a few people scatter around tables, eating. Adrian moves by the kitchen door, ready to help clean up. His appetite left him before he left the meeting room at the government agency.

“Thanks for dinner, Adrian,” Tessa says, scrapping her plate over a rubbish bin. “I’ve got a job interview tomorrow.”

Adrian takes her plate, smiling. “Wow, that’s great. Good luck.”

“Eddy helped me look through the donated clothes and I think I got a good outfit for it.” She gulps and looks at the row of trestle tables in the dining room. “I hope I get it and can move into my own place.”

“No rush, settle into the job first.”

“You’ve got enough people here to worry about.”

“Hey,” he says, resting a hand on her shoulder. “As long as we can keep this place open, you’re welcome as long as you need.”

“I’ve been here two months,” Tessa hushes. “How can you not wanna kick me out?”

Adrian laughs. “I’ve been here for three years. Should I get booted, too?”

Tessa relaxes with a smile. “C’mon, we’d all be lost without you.”

After another person scrapes their plate, Adrian ties up the rubbish bag and lifts it out of the bin. “Get a good night sleep, Tessa. You need to be fresh for the interview.”

Tessa nods, moving toward the bedrooms. “I hope these nerves let me sleep.”

“See Eddy for some meditation tips if you have trouble getting to sleep,” Adrian suggests.

“Will do.”

Adrian carries the rubbish through the kitchen and out the back door to the graffitied alley, which is littered with broken glass and illuminated by one small security light. He tosses the rubbish in the dumpster, and as he closes the lid, a garbled voice rings through the alley.

He squints as a shadowy figure stumbles around the alley. "Hello?" he calls out.

A wispy giggle echoes as the light brings the figure into focus. Adrian steps forward as a young woman wearing a red headscarf babbles slurred words.

"Miss? Are you ok?" Adrian calls out.

She hears him, because she stops dead. She slurs another sentence and then collapses to the cement.

"*Whoah*! Are you ok?" Adrian's heart thunders in his chest as he races to the girl. He skids to a stop, lowering to the ground beside her. *Uh-oh*, he thinks at the sight of her jet-black hair. "I'm sorry," he apologises in fear of disrespecting her religious beliefs.

He checks her breathing, and it patters against his cheek. He takes in a whiff of her sweet, floral perfume and notices the angles of her olive face. He chews his lips and stops himself from thinking about how pretty she is.

"Adrian? You all right?" Hector calls from the kitchen.

Adrian waves at the kitchen. "Come over and give me a hand. This girl's unconscious."

"Ah, shit," Hector yelps, racing into the alley. "Junkie?"

"Just drunk, I think," Adrian says, tucking an arm under the girl's back. Hector gets on her other side, and Adrian says, "On three. One, two, three."

They lift the young woman, with one of her arms around each of their necks. "Let's get her inside," Adrian says, tightening his hold on her and checking if she stirs awake.

They carry her through the kitchen, and Adrian tells Hector to hurry through the dining room.

"*Whoah*, who's this?" Eddy says, moving between the tables to reach them.

"C'mon Hector," Adrian says, nodding towards the bedrooms, "keep going."

They move into the hall and Tessa walks into her room.

"Tessa, can you keep the door open?" Adrian calls to her.

"Oh, sure," Tessa says, startled and backing out of the doorway. "Who is that?"

"We don't know," Hector says as they bustle into the room.

Adrian lifts the girl fully into his arms and slides her onto the bed.

"Was she in the alley?" Eddy asks, moving into the room, concern dripping off every word.

Adrian smooths down his shirt and moves from the bed. "Yeah. She was stumbling and slurring her words and then collapsed." He finds Tessa's eyes. "Sorry, d'you mind if she sleeps it off in here?"

Tessa shakes her head. "I'm sure she'll be a welcomed distraction."

Used

Jazz rubs her head, moaning as she pulls the sheets away from her face. *What happened? Why do I have such a monster headache?*

She sits up in bed, hair cascading round her face, and *clunk.*

"Ow!" she wails. She rubs her forehead and squints an eye open. Planks of wood line overhead with a mattress poking between each plank. *A bunk bed?*

"Ah, Adrian," a girl's voice calls.

Jazz pans the room to see who and where she is. The room is bleak, with a chipped dresser and scuffed walls. A girl with a spiky, pixie cut and nose ring stands by the doorway, staring at her.

"Adrian, she's up," the girl says with a jittery voice.

Jazz scrambles to the top of the bed and claws the sheets, pulling them to her neck. *I've been kidnapped!*

"Stay away from me!" Jazz yells, her limbs trembling and colour draining from her face. "Stay away. Whatever it is you think you will get from me, you won't get it!"

A man bustles into the room. "*Whoah, whoah, whoah,*" he says, hands outs like stop signs, his volume low. "You're all right. You're all right."

"You can't keep me here!" Jazz yells.

The young man smiles. "We're not interested in keeping anyone against their will. But when you walk by here drunk as a skunk, we kinda need to give ya a bed."

"What?" Jazz whispers. *Drunk?* Her mind goes into overdrive to recount last night's memories. "*Ugh.* Ethan."

"Ethan?" the young man repeats. "Is he your husband? Boyfriend? Brother?"

Jazz squints at him, taking in his shiny, brown eyes and the kind creases that tell of many smiles and laughter. "Who are you?"

"I'm Adrian," he says, kneeling by her bed. "You're at a refuge centre, a halfway house. Is it ok that I talk to you? We don't have any female staff here at the moment." He turns to pixie-cut. "Where's her headscarf?"

"Headscarf?" Jazz repeats with mild interest.

Adrian turns back. "I'm so sorry we can see your hair. Is there anything I can do to make you more comfortable or repair any religious beliefs I may have broken?"

Jazz's forehead scrunches as she takes in the sincerity in his face. She runs a hand through her unkempt hair and watches the light dance in his eyes. She looks at the dark skin of her arm and then to his fair, beige skin tone, and smiles. "I'm not Muslim."

Adrian backs up, his expression switching between confused and relieved. "Oh, you're not?"

Jazz smirks. "Not all brown people are Muslim."

"Oh no," Adrian says, standing and waving his arms, "I meant nothing disrespectful. I... I..."

Jazz smiles as he retracts his casual racism, and then something comes back to mind. "I was wearing a headscarf?"

"This thing," Pixie-cut says, lifting the alleged headscarf.

Jazz laughs. "That's a pashmina." She takes in their bewildered expressions. "A shawl. It's not a religious symbol, it's a fashion accessory."

"Oh," they both exhale, shoulders drooping.

"So we haven't offended you?" Adrian asks sheepishly.

"I'm more confused than anything," Jazz replies.

Pixie-cut walks over and hands Jazz the shawl. "I'm Tessa."

"Thanks," Jazz says, massaging the fabric with her thumbs. They both look at her expecting an introduction. Jazz introduces herself to people who already know who she is, but these two seem clueless. "You don't know who I am?"

Adrian shakes his head. "You were unconscious when we found you."

Jazz touches her cheek and leans forward. "You don't recognise me?"

"Should we?" Tessa asks.

Jazz's eyes widen, and her chin drops. *This never happens.* "I'm Jazz."

"Nice to meet you, Jazz," Adrian says. "Tessa, will you take Jazz to find some clothes?"

"Clothes?" Jazz questions.

"You wanna change out of that dress?" Adrian asks. "You slept through breakfast but the kitchen is getting lunch ready. I'll see you two in the dining room."

Adrian leaves, and Jazz slides out of bed. She gasps in horror at the state of her dress. The blue material is filthy with dirt and has rips at the knees. "My dress!"

She scoops her hair over her shoulder and closes her eyes. She shakes her head, trying to unsee it.

"You wanna brush your hair?" Tessa says by a chest of drawers, swinging her hairbrush.

"Thanks, but I don't use other people's hairbrushes."

"Girl, everything here has been used by someone else."

Jazz's jaw clenches. "Wait, are you taking me to get *used* clothes?"

Tessa nods. "They're donated by people in the community."

Jazz gulps and tries her best to remove the repulsion from her face. "Ok, let's get it over with."

"Grateful much?" Tessa smirks, leading her out of the room.

Jazz is careful going through the clothes. She selects a white t-shirt with *Baby* written in red. It smells of laundry detergent and has no stains. She finds a pair of blue jeans and hopes for the best. She asks Tessa to show her where she can shower.

The jeans are stiff to walk in as she enters the dining room with Tessa. Jazz hopes it's a good sign they weren't worn by someone else.

"Just take a seat in here," Tessa says. "I have to go to my job interview."

"Oh, what's the job?"

"It's phone support at an insurance company."

Jazz scrutinises Tessa's attire, and general appearance, and purses her lips so the wince doesn't escape. Jazz knows the interviewer will note Tessa's appearance as a negative. She already has.

"Good luck," Jazz says.

"Thank you," Tessa says, waving as she leaves the dining room.

Jazz sits at a plastic trestle table on a plastic stackable seat. Her elbows rest on the table and her fingers swipe over her eyelashes.

"You find everything ok?" Adrian asks, walking by her table.

She nods. "Yes, thank you." She reflects on the communal bathroom situation. The cracked tiles, exposed and rusted pipes, and growing mould. Yes, the showers were in their own cubicles, but that didn't stop the water from the neighbouring shower slide in and over her feet. *Gross!* "Oh, Adrian."

Adrian turns and circles back to her. "Yeah?"

"Can I have my bag?"

He shakes his head. "You didn't have a bag."

She frowns. "I didn't?"

He folds his arms and tilts his head. "Think you dropped it somewhere?"

"*Ugh*. Probably. Thanks, anyway."

Adrian smiles and moves toward the kitchen.

My phone. Jazz can go a few days, even a week or two, without checking in with her father. Not phoning him isn't an issue. *Imagine what he would think of this place.* She swallows roughly when her Collage account comes to mind. Her fingers twitch with the need to check stats and post her latest image.

She smooths her palms on the table and sighs. *Forget the phone for two seconds. I need to collect my thoughts after that disaster of a meeting with Ethan. I need to beat him.*

The hangover is getting the better of her. She sits back on the chair, air draining through her nostrils, and decides to ease into the day. After an hour of quiet, she'll head to her office to finish her proposal for the board.

Proposal. She shudders. Memories of hitting another bar after Overity and more intoxicating drinks filter into her mind. *What a mistake.*

A tubby man with a scruffy black beard waddles out of the kitchen with a tray of sandwiches. He places them on a table and meets her eyes.

"Hey homegirl," he says, waving at her.

"Me?" Jazz asks, pointing to her chest.

Tubby chuckles and moves toward her. "You wouldn't remember me. You were out cold. Adrian asked me to help bring ya in last night."

"Oh no," Jazz hushes, her reddening face collapsing in her hands.

Tubby laughs. "That's right. I'm Hector. You ain't got nothing to be embarrassed about. We seen a lot worse around here."

Jazz lifts her head. "Really?"

"Miles worse. So bad I assumed you was a junkie."

Jazz pulls back, crossing her arms. "Well, thanks."

Hector laughs. "No sweat, homegirl." He gestures to the food. "We got sandwiches for lunch, but dinner is da bomb. We go buffet-style."

"Thanks, I won't be here for—"

"—What's your name, anyways."

She stiffens. *Don't recognise me. Please, don't recognise me.* "Jazz."

"Jazz? Like the music."

She breathes out, smiling. "Yes. Like the music."

"Right on, homegirl. That's sweet." Hector waves and makes his way back to the kitchen. "Help yourself to some lunch."

Jazz stands and moves to the sandwiches. Before she can check out the selection, Adrian emerges from the kitchen with another platter. A boy of about seventeen pulls him aside to talk. Jazz notices the attentiveness in Adrian's expression and the way the kid smiles and accepts Adrian's advice.

"Hungry?" Adrian asks, walking by Jazz.

"Yes, thank you." She bites her lip and then adds, "My money would be in my bag... So I don't have any now, but I can pay later."

Adrian sits the platter on the table and shakes his head. "You don't pay for this."

"You don't?"

"We provide this for everyone," Adrian replies. "To make sure everyone eats."

"Oh." It takes a bit too long for it to sink in for Jazz.

Adrian pats her shoulder. "Don't worry. You're ok."

He thinks I'll go hungry? Jazz takes in the happiness of his disposition, the effortless waves in his light brown hair, and the robustness of his smile. A tingle runs down her spine and she blushes as she turns to the food.

"I'll catch you later," he says, and moves towards the kitchen.

Jazz shakes her shoulders, fighting the silly tingles. *A crush, Jazz? Don't be ridiculous.*

Digging

Ethan rubs a towel behind his neck and slings it over his shoulder. He walks back into his loft apartment after a vigorous session at the Ultimate ME gym on the corner. He pulls a bottle of water from the fridge and rounds the stainless steel benches, to cross the polished concrete floors to the living area.

He flops on the couch, still reeling over his meeting with Jazz. *How could she walk out on me? She ruined a bulletproof plan.* He lifts his phone, the temptation to read work emails greater than showering. He scrolls through the inbox and lands on an email titled: "Jazz Abadi Replacement."

He reads the email, which entails who will take over Jazz's duties while she is on leave. *She has taken leave?* Ethan tilts his head to view Jazz's handbag on his kitchen counter. She left it at the bar, and he took it home with him. *She didn't turn up for work. No one can reach her. Do they assume she's sick?*

A smile creeps on Ethan's face. Images of a drunken Jazz, staggering through the streets of the Nightclub District, take over his thoughts. *Ha, maybe she got run over.*

He dials a number in his contacts and places the phone to his ear.

"Yes," a voice answers.

"It's Roth," Ethan replies. "I need you to do some digging for me."

"What have you got?"

"Jazz Abadi. She's disappeared and I need you to locate her."

"There's a missing person alert on her?"

"No, not yet, and I need it to stay that way. Find her and keep it on the down-low." Ethan eyes Jazz's phone. "Also, I need you to hack into her phone. I'll send you the details. I need to access the contents and disarm the tracking."

"So, Miss Abadi doesn't have her phone, you do?"

"*Ignacio*," Ethan snaps. "I'm paying you to do my dirty work. Don't mess with me. Jazz was last seen at Overity. She left her bag behind. I have her phone, and I need access. Make it happen."

"Ok, ok, I'll get right on it," Officer Ignacio replies timidly.

"Pull the security footage from Overity. Wipe it from the bar's hard drive and send me everything."

"Yes, Sir. Will do."

Ethan ends the call with the police officer. He stares at Jazz's phone and smiles. *Time to get to work.*

"Good morning, Darius," Ethan says, smoothing his suit jacket as he strides into his soon-to-be office.

"Morning," Darius says with a mediocre wave from behind his desk. His forehead rests in his palm as he reads over paperwork.

"I saw Jazz is on leave," Ethan says, unbuttoning his jacket and sitting on an armchair across from Darius. "Thought she might be here by your side."

"Haven't heard from her." Darius clears his throat, lifts his head and straightens his tie. "I'm sure she's diligently working on her presentation and will be in soon."

"That's what I would have thought," Ethan says, pulling out his phone. He slides the phone towards Darius, opened to a text from Jazz. *Boarding a yacht to do some island-hopping. Need some time away to recharge.* "Looks serious, huh?"

Darius frowns at the text message. "This is from Jazz?"

"It's her number, isn't it?" Ethan replies, relaxing in his seat. "Once a socialite, always a socialite."

Grimacing, Darius pushes the phone toward Ethan. The desk phone rings, and Darius lifts the receiver to take the call.

Ethan pockets his phone. The text from Ignacio replays in his mind. *Jazz Abadi added to her tab at Sako Bar after leaving Overity last night. A woman matching her description was seen at the marina in the early hours of the morning. Still tracing her whereabouts.*

He slips out Jazz's phone from the other side of his jacket. He crafts a message to Darius. *Father, I'm getting away with some girlfriends. I can't do this anymore. I need some fun in my life.*

Darius stands from his desk chair with the landline receiver clutched between his shoulder and cheek. He paces as he pulls his mobile phone from his pocket.

Ethan watches Darius' face droop as he reads over Jazz's text. Ethan combs his fingers through his sandy blonde hair, trying to distract himself from smiling. He clears his throat and sits up straight as Darius ends his call.

"Everything ok?" Ethan says, pinching the crease of his pant leg.

"Heather was just scheduling a meeting," Darius says, acknowledging the desk phone.

Ethan smiles at Darius as warmly as he can muster. "I was referring to the other phone. I saw your reaction. Let me guess: Jazz?"

Darius paces by his bookshelf and pans the row of photos showing his business endeavours and a few posed with his daughter. "It's not important."

Ethan stands and re-buttons his jacket. "She's not serious about the company.”

Darius turns to Ethan, apprehension sinking into his face. “She’s always worked here.”

Ethan exhales and broaches the topic slowly. “We met last night for drinks. She confided in me.”

“Confided?”

Ethan lowers his gaze and tries for an empathetic look. “She told me she resents the Abadi name.” He looks up and meets Darius’ reddened eyes. “She doesn’t care for you, Sir.”

Darius clutches his heart and anchors his other hand on the bookshelf. “No. No, that can’t be.”

“I’m sorry, Darius,” Ethan says, closing in on him. “She’s not here for you. Not like I am.”

Darius clicks his finger towards his desk. “My pills. My pills.”

Ethan rushes to the desk and picks up a pill bottle. He skims the instructions, tips two pills out, and pours a glass of water from the bar in the corner. He takes it to Darius, who washes them down.

Darius hands the glass back to Ethan with a shaky hand. “Thank you, Son.”

A smile curls Ethan’s lips. “You’re more than welcome. I’m always here for you.”

Ethan helps Darius back to his desk. He stands by him as Darius works, asking about his day-to-day routine and being the world’s best mentee.

Ethan notices the way Darius sighs between tasks. His thoughts drifting with the knowledge Jazz is off with her friends and has little care for her ailing father.

Ethan demonstrates a new way to incorporate a flowchart to monitor staff productivity, displaying himself as the prodigal son and rightful heir who cares about the running of the company.

“I can’t believe that Jazz would leave at a time like this,” Darius says with a sigh.

Ethan ignores the comment and continues to explain how his idea will push the company forward.

"She knows how important this is," Darius says, lost in his thoughts. "There must be something terribly wrong."

Ethan groans, slamming his hands on the desk and rounding to face Darius. "How about you focus on me right now? I'm the one here and committed to the company." His cheeks redden as the anger swells inside him. "I'm not the vain socialite who spends her time posting to her social media feed."

"Compose yourself, Roth," Darius says. "She's the social media marketer for the company. Her Collage feed is for the business."

Ethan sighs, stepping back from the desk. "My apologies. I'm just worried about Jazz."

"How so?"

"There's something wrong with her," Ethan says, lowering to meet Darius eye-to-eye. "Maybe mentally? She was extremely aggressive to me last night."

Darius sits back, shocked. "What?"

"She got drunk and hurled abuse at me. I tried to help her, but she got physical with me."

"There is nothing wrong with my daughter's mental faculties. She's an intelligent young woman."

"She's brilliant... when sober." Ethan pulls out his phone and opens Collage. "Did you see these photos? Some were taken by paparazzi, others from the general public in the Nightclub District. This was Jazz last night. She could barely stand."

Darius frowns, shakes his head, and looks away.

Ethan takes his phone, sits down, and lowers his voice to add, "Darius, I think you need to think about a rehab facility instead of a CEOship for Jazz."

Darius' jaw drops. Colour drains from his face as he slowly shakes his head, unable to fathom the claims. Darius' declining health hinders his strong mind, allowing him to become malleable to Ethan's manipulations.

"You should have seen the amount of drinks she had," Ethan says in a low voice. "And now she's on a yacht to continue her alcoholism? I think there's something deeply troubling Jazz that we haven't picked up on. Maybe from her childhood? Her mother?"

An incoming message pings on Ethan's phone. It's a video file from Officer Ignacio with the following text: ***Overity footage. No sound. Agitated Abadi.*** Ethan locks his phone, weighing up his options. Leak it to the press, or just the members of the board?

Darius smooths a hand over his greying hair. The wrinkles on his face deepen somehow. "Jazz and I don't have the best communication when it comes to non-business matters. We will wait for her to explain herself."

Ethan crosses his legs and clasps his hands. He taps his fingers between his knuckles, distracting himself enough to hide his smile.

Dirty

Jazz stands against a dining room wall, her hands clasped in front, as she watches people pass her by.

"You look lost," Adrian says, approaching her.

"Oh, do I?" Jazz asks, straightening her stance.

"Have you met Eddy?"

"Eddy?"

"Our counsellor. If there's any stuff you need to talk about, you can talk with him. It's all private."

She shakes her head. "Oh. No, I'm ok."

"Well, he'll be around, anyway." Adrian shrugs. "I'll introduce you if we pass him. You wanna come with me?"

"Where are you going?" she asks with mild curiosity.

"Lunch was quiet today, so they don't need me to help clean up. I'm gonna check on the rest of our supplies." He nods to the hall. "I can give ya a tour."

Jazz pushes off the wall. "Sure, I'd love a tour."

"Great," he says with a bright smile.

"So, you don't charge for the counselling either?" Jazz asks, a half-step behind him.

"What do you mean?"

"You give everything away for free?"

"Yeah, we're not-for-profit. We're here to help those in need." Adrian nods to a man passing them in the hall. "Hey Tim."

Jazz looks Tim up and down. Scruffy hair, overgrown beard, untucked and crinkled button-down shirt, ripped hem of faded chinos.

"But what about your staff?" Jazz asks. "You pay them. How do you pay them without an income?"

"Most people here are volunteers. They have other jobs where they get paid."

"They work a second job where they don't get paid?"

"That's what volunteering is."

"Ok. Sorry, I've never seen how anything like this works. I've only seen things from a retail perspective."

"You work in retail?"

"A family business," Jazz blurts to skirt the issue.

"Ah, stuff with families can be tough, huh?"

"I guess."

Adrian stops at a T in the hall. "So, you know this side. This is our female and families' end, and on the right are the male bedrooms and bathrooms. We keep them separate because we have women who come from abuse and aren't comfortable around men." He meets Jazz's eyes. "But you have nothing to worry about. Everyone is looking for the same thing here. Comfort, respect, and safety."

"I look worried?"

"You have the same look everyone has when they get here. Plus, you mentioned a male name when you woke up this morning."

Jazz sniggers. "Please, Ethan isn't a threat to me."

Adrian nods with apprehension seeping across his face.

He doesn't believe me. He thinks I'm a battered woman.

As Adrian checks the bathroom supplies, Jazz takes in the women and young children mingling in the hall. Her stomach jitters as she swallows uncomfortably. She can't put her finger on it. There's something consistent about all the people here. *Dirty*. They are all dishevelled. Dirt seems impossible to remove from their faces, hands, and clothes.

Jazz presses her fingers firmly into her stomach. She has never interacted with a busker or beggar on the streets, and now she's surrounded by them. *Where did I wake up?*

"Where is this place?" she asks Adrian.

Adrian turns to her, stacking towels. "You mean the address?"

Jazz takes a step back, hugging her mid-section. "Am I still in Maiden City?"

Adrian meets her eyes. "Yes, you're in Maiden City. We are on Jordan Street, below the Nightclub District."

Jazz's eyebrows lift. "How far below?"

"The Limits start behind us. It was the best location we could get."

Jazz sighs and gazes at the size-too-big flip flops on her feet. "I didn't get too far from the bar then."

"You remember where you were last night?"

She nods.

"Anything you wanna talk about?" he asks.

She keeps eyes on her bare toes. "No, thank you."

"Our location may not be the best, but most people who need our help come from The Limits. So, our location is a godsend for them. The closer to the city limits, the harder life can get."

"I heard they're trying to shut down that part of the city."

Adrian's jaw clenches. "Probably so the rich can flatten the homes and build factories, or something."

Jazz senses some hostility and decides not to continue on the topic. Sovereign Hill, where she is from, is on the opposite side of the city and is viewed as the top end of town.

Adrian shows Jazz through the male quarters, and even though he said it was safe, she averts her eyes. *Why am I still in this place?* She makes her mind actively work on her presentation for the board. The need to be CEO of Ultimate ME never greater.

No one in this forgotten place comes to her with problems to solve. For once she can concentrate on her work without someone else interfering. She can focus her mind on climbing the corporate ladder and finally claiming her father's approval.

"And down here is the common room," Adrian says, gesturing to a sizeable room with couches and a pool table. "It's mostly where the kids hangout, but it's nice for anyone to come and chill. We have random movies and board games if you wanna spend some time in here."

Jazz jolts out of her thoughts. The room is dismal, even with curtains open. The couches faded and torn. Sad books lay on the coffee table, and clutter piles in every corner. *People live this way?* Something pricks behind Jazz's eyes. Her mind goes to her expansive bedroom and to the entertainment theatre on the lower level of the Abadi Mansion. *How can I have so much, and others share so little? This is the best they have?*

She sniffs hard, and asks, "Is there anything I can do to help?"

Adrian tilts his head to view her. "What's that?"

"Around here?" Jazz gestures to the room and the hall. "Is there anything I can do to help? Maybe I can start with cleaning?"

Adrian's smile lights up the dim room. "Sure, that'd be great."

Wronged

Adrian looks at her sideways. *Who is this mysterious girl?* At first, he thought Jazz had run from abuse, but she struts around the shelter with an independent confidence. Jazz doesn't seem to need help or is unwilling to take it. *Did she come from harm, or not?*

It touched Adrian when Jazz offered to help. The chore list is forever mounting. He never expected her to be so much work. He wipes his brow, stemming frustration as the glint in her eyes tells of more burning questions.

"Are you sure you want me to start with the floors?" she asks, her raven hair cascading down her left shoulder, as her chin tilts upward.

Adrian folds his arm across his middle. "What now?"

"Well," Jazz drags the word. "Wouldn't it be better to clean the tables and chairs first? That way any debris that falls to the floor wouldn't ruin the effort put into cleaning the floors."

Seriously, who is she? She talks so differently to everyone else here. He assigned her the floors because it was the longest chore he could think of. "Sure, Jazz, do the chairs and tables first, and then the floors."

Jazz grins and spins toward the cleaning closet.

Adrian sighs and shakes his head, walking towards the boys' bedrooms. Every task he gives Jazz, she questions. First, she questions why it's done, then she wants to change the process. "To be more productive," she would say.

Adrian stretches his arms high, tilting his head side-to-side. *Just let her go, Adrian. It's gotta be helping her cope.*

Arguing echoes through the hall from a bedroom. Adrian rushes to the room. "You boys ok?"

DJ pushes past Adrian in the doorway and storms into the hall.

"Hey," Adrian calls after DJ. He looks inside the bedroom to Max and Ferg sitting on a lower bunk. "Guys, what's going on?"

The boys point to the hall. "He started it."

Adrian peers over his shoulder, but DJ is gone. He clenches his jaw and circles back to the common room.

"Can't you see there's a pile of dirt and rubbish there," Jazz scolds, hands on her hips, glaring at DJ. "Why did you walk through it?"

Adrian sees the messed-up pile on the floor with a shoe imprint. He blows out a breath and raises a palm toward Jazz.

He moves to the couch by DJ. "Deej. What happened?"

"He's a rotten boy who can't—"

"*Jazz,*" Adrian cuts her off, nostrils flaring as he shoots her a look.

Jazz's face grows a shade lighter. She takes a step back and wipes the TV cabinet.

Adrian takes another inhale, internally counting to three like Eddy taught him. "DJ. You were getting along so well with Max and Ferg."

DJ hugs himself tight, frowning. "No I never."

Adrian tries to ignore Jazz's groan. "Can you guys work this out, or do I have to reassign rooms?"

DJ snatches the TV remote from the coffee table and clicks the TV on.

Adrian huffs and sits back on the couch, turning his attention to the TV. "You used to talk to me."

Jazz cleans the same part of the TV cabinet multiple times, lips purse like she's begging to say something.

DJ flicks through the stations until he finally chucks the remote on the table and groans. "They were just leaving me out."

"Leaving you out?"

"They're just jerks," DJ hisses, getting up and leaving the room.

"DJ," Adrian calls as he leans forward for the remote. He points the remote at the TV but doesn't click the power button when he notices Jazz is fixated on the screen.

"Experts tip Ethan Roth as the front runner to take control of Ultimate ME Fitness Group. Shareholders are waiting with bated breath on this one," a news reporter on screen says. "And in other finance news..."

Adrian lowers the remote, taken by the concern covering her face. "You ok?"

Jazz jumps as if she forgot he was there. She moves to a bookshelf and hurriedly wipes down the shelf. "Yep, I'm fine."

Adrian turns the TV off and moves from the couch. "You're doing good in here. Just lay off the kid."

"You ever heard of that company?" Jazz asks the book spines.

"What company?"

"The one the reporter mentioned."

"Oh. No. Why?"

She grumbles and shakes it off. "Nothing."

Adrian nods, clenching his jaw, and backs to the doorway. "I'll be back to check on you soon."

Jazz bats a hand in a pathetic wave, and Adrian tries not to decode the subtext.

Jazz is still antsy at dinner, so Adrian politely suggests she helps with meal service. Something about her upright and tense posture tells him this girl needs to be doing something every waking moment.

His eyes fixate on her as she hands out plates. Something is so off about her. Her mannerisms are formal. She eyes everyone with distrust. Either she talks down to people, or she impresses them with the high-class service of a fancy restaurant.

Adrian rubs the stubble sprouting along his jawline and squeezes his eyes closed. *I can't watch anymore.*

He opens his eyes and huffs. He slides across to Jazz and pushes gently on the plate in her hand. "Can I talk to you for a minute?"

Jazz returns the plate to the stack and nods.

Adrian beckons her to a corner and folds his arms. "You don't have to try so hard, you know."

Her chin drops and her eyes dart side-to-side. "What are you talking about?"

"Helping out," Adrian says, gesturing to the buffet. "You don't have to act a certain way. Just relax. No one expects anything grand. Be natural."

Her eyebrow lifts. "Natural?"

"Yeah." Adrian smiles. "You don't have to pretend to be someone you're not. Everyone is free to be themselves here."

Just when Adrian thinks she might loosen up, a scowl crosses Jazz's face. "You think I'm being fake?"

Adrian raises his hand defensively. "No, that's not what I'm saying. You just have a fish-outta-water vibe. Where did you live before coming here?"

Jazz's shoulders droop and she takes a step away from him. Her eyes shine like a tear might drop. "Can you excuse me? I need to go to the bathroom." Her frown is iron-clad as she moves to the doorway.

"Yeah, sure, no worries," Adrian says, feeling two-feet tall. He rubs his head. *Geez, who wronged this girl?*

Forbidden

"**Jazz**, are you able to help in the kitchen?" Adrian asks as Jazz returns to the dining room.

"In the kitchen?" Jazz didn't mean for the hesitation to slip out in her voice. She locks eyes with Adrian and shivers run down her arms. Her gaze plummets to the floor, her jaw flexes, and she internally scolds herself.

"Yeah, I need to make a phone call," Adrian says, approaching her. "It's just washing a few dishes. Eddy is inside to show you the ropes."

Jazz nods, her cheeks burning. *Abadi, pull yourself together.* "Not a problem."

Adrian smiles, and lines crinkle by his brightening brown eyes. "Thanks, I appreciate it so much."

Adrian moves out of the dining room, and Jazz studies the strange feeling rushing through her body. *A crush?* Jazz groans and shakes her shoulders. She's never let herself feel something so stupid before. Romance is a deadly distraction. It takes so many business women's eyes off the prize when they let it consume them. Jazz needs to compete like a man. Silly little crushes are a weakness and need to be killed and buried as soon as they bloom.

Why is she feeling this way towards him, anyway? *He accused me of being fake. The only proper way to interact with people is with decorum and professionalism. Sure, I'm not being forthcoming with my identity, but neither are others around here. Or is it only ok when they do it?*

Is it the fact she thought about him in that forbidden way that made her so upset? She bites into her bottom lip, taking a moment to feel the warmth under her skin. It is his darn smile. It's magnetising. It's hard to stay mad at him.

Jazz snaps out of her thoughts and rushes towards the kitchen. She pushes the door open and a tall, slim man with side-swept dark blonde hair, slender green eyes and high cheekbones greets her.

He smiles, drying a plate. "Hey there. You're Jazz?"

She steps into the kitchen, panning across the greasy stove top, stainless steel troughs and three jam-packed rubbish bins. "Yes, that's me. Eddy?"

He places the plate on a stack and wipes his hand against the dish towel. He extends his hand towards her. "That's me. Good to meet you."

Jazz looks between the almost-rag-towel and his hand. She sucks in a breath and shakes his hand. "You too."

Eddy whips the towel over his shoulder and gestures around the room. "Welcome to the kitchen. It's not in the greatest shape right now. The dishwasher broke down a few weeks ago, so we need to wash everything by hand. Yes, it is as fun as it sounds."

He waits for Jazz to laugh. She stares at him with bewildered eyes, wondering what exactly she has to do.

"Hector got through all the pots and pans. We just have the plates and cups left. You want to wash or dry?"

Jazz peers into the sudsy trough. By the white bubbles are patches of murky water and floating food scraps. She nods at the stack of plates. "Dry. If you don't mind?"

Eddy hands her the towel, smiling. "Totally fine with me."

"Thanks," Jazz says, pinching the edge of the damp towel.

Eddy slides his hands into the water, nodding towards the corner. There are other towels in the crate down there, if that one is too wet."

Jazz moves to the crate. "Thank you."

"So, how are you doing?" Eddy asks, eyes focused on the plate he's scrubbing.

"Fine," Jazz replies slowly, shoulders closing in.

Eddy hands her the plate while grabbing for the next. "I'm the counsellor here, so if there's anything you need to discuss, we can have a sit down and—"

"—Uh, no, I'm fine," she cuts him off.

"It's just if you need to unburden."

"I don't believe in therapy."

"Everyone who comes here is running from something." He looks over his shoulder at her. "Do you know what it is you're running from?"

Her lip upturns as her head jerks back. "I'm not running from anything." Eddy's eyebrows lift and she composes her posture. "I'm waiting."

Eddy turns back to the sink. "You're sure?"

"Yes, of course. So, counsellor and kitchenhand?"

"We all help in any area that needs pitching in. Hector and Maria had to leave early tonight. I don't mind staying back late."

"Well, that's quite nice."

"Just keep what I said in mind," he says, scrubbing against the water. "My door is always open if it gets too much."

"There's nothing to uncover. I'm not like everyone else here."

Eddy looks over his shoulder again, and there's something in his eyes that makes her audibly gulp. She shakes her shoulders and flashes a Collage-worthy smile.

A limp smile curves his lips, and he returns his attention to the sink.

45

Circumstances

Jazz lifts herself out of bed after another night on the bottom bunk's much-too-soft and lumpy mattress. She stretches her back and neck and decides it's time to return to the real world.

She combs her hair with her fingers, avoiding the brush Tessa kindly offered. She'll go to the gym in the second-hand jeans and tee, knowing she has a change of clothes and clean shower waiting for her there.

She makes her way to the dining room, hoping to find fruit to take with her to the gym.

"Morning, Jazz," Adrian says, waving from a table with a woman and her child sitting beside him.

Jazz nods, her smile curving before she can hide it. "Good morning."

Adrian turns back to the woman, lowering his voice as he talks to her.

Jazz moves to the food and keeps her gaze low on the pair. The woman's olive face is shadowed by the hood of her sweatshirt. Dark bags hang under her eyes and her black as night hair falls beside her face, escaping her hood. As Jazz takes in the woman's features, her chest constricts, and she draws in shallow breaths. Despite the hardships worn on the woman's face, she looks so much like Jazz. With a different set of circumstances, it could be Jazz sitting there, broken and scared.

Jazz looks to the toddler on the woman's lap. Tired red lines mark his shiny round eyes against his dark skin. Jazz sucks back a breath as her eyes sting and water. She squeezes her eyes shut and opens them to clear vision.

"Morning," Tessa says, moving away with her breakfast plate.

"Good morning," Jazz says. "Hey, how did your job interview go?"

Tessa shrugs, faking a smile. "It was good. It was short. Is that a good or bad sign?"

Bad. "Maybe they didn't need that much time because they knew you'd be a great fit."

Tessa's posture lifts, and her smile grows. "Thanks, Jazz."

"No problem," Jazz whispers as Tessa moves to a table. She scratches her head, wondering if she should be more honest with Tessa, or would it damage her more?

How is she damaged in the first place?

She looks across the tables in the dining room and the scattering of people. *How did any of them get here?* She focuses on Adrian and the woman and child next to him. Her gut quivers as she snatches a banana and apple and moves over to their table.

She sits a few chairs away as she notices how fragile the woman is and how quietly Adrian is talking to her. His mannerisms are so gentle, and Jazz fixates on the calm movements of his hands and the softness of his lips as he whispers.

Adrian picks up a piece of toast, and as he takes a bite, his eyes meet Jazz's. Jazz jumps in her seat like she was caught spying. Adrian smiles awkwardly as he chews. He swallows roughly and nods at her. "You ok?"

"Mhmm," she blurts, peeling the banana.

He gestures to the seat opposite him. "You wanna move closer?"

The pace of Jazz's heartbeat quickens as she eyes the sad woman.

"It's ok," Adrian adds.

Jazz picks up her fruit and moves across the two empty seats to the one opposite Adrian.

"You sleep ok?" he asks, taking another bite of buttered toast.

"Had things on my mind," she says to the table so to not eye the woman.

"Anything you want to talk about?" Adrian says to his plate. "Did Eddy—"

"—I'm ok," Jazz interrupts. "It's just work stuff."

Adrian looks up with surprise shining in his eyes. "Your family's business?"

Jazz's mouth drops and she leans back in her chair, bundling her hair to the right. "I don't really want to talk about it."

Adrian's smile is small, but just as warm. He looks to the woman with the child. "This is Myra and Taz."

Myra fidgets in her seat, hugging the child closer. Taz turns in her arms, courageously smiling at Jazz.

Jazz's heart swells as she takes in the child's sweet yet dirty face.

"They just got here this morning," Adrian says, letting Taz high-five his palm. "Myra and Taz, this is Jazz."

Myra flicks her eyes up to take in Jazz, and quickly lowers her head again. Jazz realises why no one has recognised her. They barely look up.

"Hi Myra," Jazz begins, but halts her sentence when realising how inappropriate it would be to ask, 'how are you.' She looks to Taz again and finds herself grinning. "Hey there, little one."

Adrian slides back in his seat and asks Jazz, "D'you mind keeping them company for a minute? There's just someone else I need to check on."

Jazz's heartbeat is in her ears as her face flushes with heat. "Sure. Not a problem."

"I'll be right back," Adrian whispers to Myra, who doesn't lift her head.

As Adrian moves away, Taz squeaks with despair, throwing his hand out, wanting to keep high-fiving.

"Here, here," Jazz says, sending her arm across the table for Taz to hit. She watches Myra settle in her seat and she asks, "He's your son?"

Myra tightens her arms around Taz and nods. "Yes, he's mine."

Jazz frowns at Myra's insecure body language. Keeping her arm outstretched for Taz, she moves a seat over to be opposite Myra. "Did someone try to take him away from you?"

Myra winces and moves her face to the left. Jazz angles her face to keep a view of Myra. Myra turns her face right and Jazz gasps at the large purple bruise under her eye and across her cheek.

"Someone hit you?" Jazz exclaims. Silence sweeps around them and she lowers her shoulders, whispering, "Sorry."

Myra nods and whispers, "We needed to escape."

Jazz watches Myra nudge her son. "His father?"

Myra locks eyes with Jazz for the first time, and mouths with her dry and cracked lips, 'Bad man.'

Jazz swallows dryly.

"Your hair is out," Myra says.

Jazz tilts her head. "Come again?"

Myra tugs at her hood. "You don't cover?"

Jazz catches on. "Oh, I'm not Muslim. I'm Jewish, but I have done nothing religious since my bat mitzvah. Are you uncomfortable?"

"My boyfriend is Christian, so I haven't practiced in a long time. But I want to go back to my community, my people."

"I have something that could help. Do you want to come to my room with me? It's ok." Jazz follows Myra's eyes to Taz. "He'll be ok."

Myra nods, bringing Taz close to her chest as she stands. "Ouch," Myra winces, falling back to her seat.

Jazz rushes to Myra's side. "Are you ok?"

Myra releases Taz and rubs her side. "I'm ok. It's just a bruise."

"We don't have to move."

"I need to fix my hair."

Jazz rubs her lips together, edging closer. "I can take him. If you're comfortable."

Myra's body language tightens, and she sucks in another painful breath. She nods. "You can take him."

Jazz smiles at the child. "Taz, you want to come with me?"

Taz turns towards Jazz with arms open. Jazz giggles, pulling the boy into her arms. "Aren't you the sweetest? How old are you?"

A confused look takes over Taz's face as he searches his mother for an answer.

Myra pulls herself up, bracing with gritted teeth. "He's two and a half."

"Wow," Jazz says with extra enthusiasm as she carries Taz towards the doorway. "You are becoming a big boy."

Taz giggles and plays with Jazz's hair.

"Do you know what rhyming is?" Jazz asks. "You hear our names? Jazz and Taz. They rhyme."

Taz laughs again. *"Taz Jazz. Taz Jazz."*

Jazz laughs, cuddling him. "That's right. Taz Jazz." Jazz slows her walk to keep with Myra's laboured pace. "How did you come up with his name?"

"I planned to name him after my father; Tazbir. But I liked Taz more, and it means crown jewel in Arabic, which I thought was cool."

"It's a well-suited name for this little man." Jazz smiles at the toddler hugged against her body. "My father did a similar thing when naming me. He wanted to name me after my mother but ended up naming me after her talent instead."

"What do you mean?"

"My mother was an incredible jazz musician. My father said thinking about her music or listening to it was the most peaceful times of his life."

"Does she still play?"

Jazz clears her throat while lifting Taz higher in her arms. "She died giving birth to me."

Myra gasps, clasping a hand to her mouth. "I am so sorry."

Jazz shakes her shoulders, flashing her Collage smile. "It's fine. It was a long time ago."

Myra's brow furrows as her eyes seek an answer. She meets Jazz's eyes and her mouth falls open. "Jazz? You're the rich girl from the fitness company?"

"*Shoosh*," Jazz hushes, taking Myra's hands. "Please don't tell anyone."

"But what are you doing here?"

"I'm just lying low as I think of a plan to counter the man trying to steal my company. It's a long story about how I ended up here, but no one has recognised me. Please don't tell anyone."

Myra nods. "I won't. Of course." A cheeky smile plays at her lips. "I've just always kinda worshipped you."

Jazz releases Myra's hands with a nervous laugh. "Worshipped?"

"I watch you on Collage. I love seeing someone who looks like me doing so well."

Jazz smiles and nods. "Things like that make my father very happy." Jazz can't help wanting to know more about Myra. "So, your boyfriend is white? That's why you were ok talking to Adrian?"

"He was so manipulative. I couldn't be there anymore. He took me away from everyone I knew." Myra smooths over Taz's hair. "And now that this one is getting older and understanding things, I couldn't keep him around that life."

"You are so brave," Jazz says, showing them into the room.

"I was stupid to wait this long."

Jazz lowers Taz to the ground. She rubs Myra's arm. "You are incredible. You took action. You are in control of your mind and body. And you're a protector of your child. You are a hero."

Myra smiles, eyeing Taz running between the bunks. "I thought I was doing the right thing keeping him with his father."

"I suppose he was a good guy when you met."

Myra nods, tears forming in her eyes. "One of the best. I can't believe how quickly everything changed."

Myra rubs her wrist whilst deep in thought, and Jazz sees the surrounding bruising. Her stomach knots as she imagines the horrific abuse Myra has come from.

Jazz moves to the foot of her bunk where her less-than-perfect dress lays, and picks up her pashmina. "You can wear this over your hair."

Myra's chin drops and eyes round. "That's gorgeous. It would have cost you so much. No. No, I can't take it."

"Please," Jazz says, moving towards Myra. "It was a gift to me and I have others at home." She sighs, eyes watering. "I have too many things at home. Please. Please take it."

Myra lets herself smile and shrugs. "Well, sure. It's very beautiful."

"There are donated clothes here. Do you want new clothes and a shower?"

Myra pulls at her hoody and laughs. "I smell, huh?"

Jazz laughs with a mix of nerves and relief. "I can show you to them and help you cover your hair."

Myra pulls Jazz close, pressing her hands firmly into her back. "Thank you, Jazz. You are an angel."

Jazz's eyes fill with tears. She blinks them away, but they refill. As she pulls out of the hug, she sniffs and wipes her face. "Oh, it's nothing. I feel like I should do more for you.”

Myra squeezes her hand. “You have nothing to make up for.”

Jazz shows Myra to the donated clothes, holding Taz’s hand, his curiosity too high to be carried. Looking at the clothes rack, Jazz mulls over her life of tending to the upper class and having a picture-perfect life on social media. Looking and acting a certain way to be accepted. The people in the shelter have nothing and are happy with the smallest gesture. There’s more to life than ‘looking good.’ So many people are in need.

As Myra looks for something modest in her size, Adrian stops by them. “You guys ok?”

With the weight of her emotion hunching her back, Jazz moves to Adrian. “She’s just going to get cleaned up.”

“Thanks for helping out with them.”

Jazz rubs between her eyes. “In another life, she could be me.”

“Sometimes we don’t pick our circumstances.”

Jazz lowers her hands and looks him in the eyes. “But we can change them. I want to help her.” She smiles at Taz. “Help them. What else can I do around here to help more?”

Adrian relaxes his posture, smiling and keeping eye contact with her. “I’m sure you have lots to offer.”

Abandon

Ethan's spit flies out of his mouth as he yells into his phone. "Why haven't you found her?"

"I'm doing the best I can," Officer Ignacio replies. "I'm still doing my rounds and trying to keep everything covert. I got you phone access and the surveillance footage."

"I need to know where she is," Ethan says, heat rising from his collar as he paces the empty board room at Ultimate ME Head Quarters. "I need to stay three steps ahead of her. What if she's coming back into the building with a plan to topple me?"

"You don't have to worry about that," Ignacio says. "The Mayor gave you the numbers. There's no way you can't stay ahead with that information."

"Just find her now!"

Ethan groans and ends the call. Jazz was giving him more work than he bargained for. He leaves the board room and crosses the executive floor to Darius' office, an updated employee policy in hand as an excuse to check in.

In Darius' office, his secretary Heather leans beside him at his desk, scrolling through her phone, whispering.

"Am I interrupting something?" Ethan asks, walking towards the desk. "I was just on the phone with Garth Cunningham from Primary Packing. They were thinking of terminating their Employees' Fitness Scheme. I told him to sit tight, and we'd sweeten the pot. Easy to accomplish, if and when I'm named CEO."

"Yes, indeed. We can't lose the Primary Packing account. That's been very lucrative since you brought them over." Darius waves away his secretary. "Thank you, Heather, that'll be all."

Heather walks by Ethan and asks, "Can I get you anything, Mr Roth?"

"No, I'm fine, thank you," Ethan says with a wink.

"Heather was just showing me Jazz's Collage page," Darius says, as Heather blushes her way out of the room. "You know I don't get into that stuff, but I know Jazz is very present on there."

"Sure," Ethan says, relaxing on a high-backed leather armchair. "She's head of social media for Ultimate ME. *Hashtag Persian Heiress*. Social media is her life."

Darius raises his palms. "But she's not on there."

Ethan rubs his clean-shaven chin roughly as he sees where this is going.

"Jazz hasn't texted me since boarding the yacht. She has not answered any of my calls. Not even a photo on Collage of her on the boat."

"Darius, her feed is about healthy living and fitness. She won't publicise she's gone on a bender. It wouldn't be very on brand."

"Who are these girlfriends she left with?" Darius asks, perplexity deepening his wrinkles. "I don't know any friends of Jazz. She told me she didn't have time for acquaintances outside of business meetings and corporate events."

"We always want our parents to be proud," Ethan says, eyes drifting around the room. "We hide the things we are ashamed of."

"Ashamed?" Darius stands and moves to the window, crossing his arms. "It's very odd. Something is not right."

"Because she's not fooling you with the perfect daughter act. Now she's letting her true self show. Did Heather show you the trending photo of her coming out of the bar? I told you, Sir, she needs help. Have you looked into a rehabilitation centre?"

Darius turns from the window, his face creased with concern. "No, something has gone awry. It's not like her to cut off all communication. Something has gone wrong on the boat. Foul play or..." Darius races to the desk phone, picking it up and stabbing number keys. "Or kidnapping. I need to talk to the police immediately."

Ethan launches from the chair and slams his hand on the switch hook, ending the call.

"What are you doing?" Darius asks, face reddening.

"Calm down, Darius," Ethan says, straightening out his blazer. "You need to focus on work. That's what I came in here to talk to you about. Focus on me."

Darius' grip around the handset tightens and his jaw rocks. "I know my daughter."

Frustration boils inside Ethan and he slams his hands on the desk, yelling, "She left because she doesn't love you!"

Darius drops the phone, clutching his heart. Colour drains from his face as sounds try to come out his mouth. "Wh... Wh... What?"

"She's not the one you should focus on," Ethan yells, looming over Darius. "You've been a father figure to me. Why won't you act like it now? I'm here, standing in front of you, but what? You want to pine for a daughter who spat on your name and abandoned everything you gave her? What about me, Darius? I thought you said you'd show me that not all parents abandon their kids?"

Darius rubs his chest, and with a raspy voice says, "You know I won't abandon you."

"Step up," Ethan urges. "The board won't accept Jazz. We already know this. Back me."

Darius blinks rapidly, his hand digging into his chest. He gasps for air and he collapses to his knees. He gasps again, face-planting the carpet.

Ethan fixes his tie, studying the limp body of his mentor. *Why must everyone make me yell?* He mulls over his options, moving towards the bar and pouring himself a single-malt scotch. He takes a sip and ponders the simplicity of taking Darius out of the equation. He'd lose the charade with Jazz and concentrate on his presentation. He takes another sip and nods to himself, knowing it will be easier to have Darius recommend his succession to the board. He finishes the scotch, returns the glass, and runs a hand in his hair to ruin the neatness.

"Heather!" he yells, moving to Darius' side. "Heather! Get help!"

Heather rushes into the office. "What's happened?"

"Call an ambulance!" Ethan says, on the ground with two fingers to Darius' pulse. "He's had a heart attack."

"Oh my lord," Heather says, quick to tears.

Heather rushes out of the office and Ethan rolls Darius over. *He's breathing.* Ethan smirks at his ageing mentor. "Just hold on a little longer. Just a few more days is all I need."

When the paramedics arrive and check Darius' vitals, Ethan's mind wanders to his game plan. Jazz was a piece on the chessboard taken out early. Darius' piece almost suffered the same fate. He needed him to cooperate, to keep everything on track.

Work with me, Darius.

Burden

Adrian's stomach churns. "I'm sorry, we don't have room," he tells a needy man who turns away from the shelter. He told him to try the church nearby, but he knows they recently hit capacity. Adrian just hopes they have generous parishioners.

Adrian takes his bags of kitchen supplies and food in through the back door of the kitchen. He leaves them for Maria to put away and drags himself to his office.

"Adrian."

He wipes slick sweat from his forehead, not looking for the face belonging to the voice. "What?"

"You said you would play pool with me."

Adrian frowns, his jaw tightening. It's Max. He did promise. But it's the last thing on his mind. He keeps walking and bats an arm behind him. "Not now."

He closes his office door behind him and his skin chills with a sickly shiver. He spent more money than he budgeted for and he's too afraid to look at what's left in the funds. He sits at the desk and claps his hands over his nose, blowing out a hard breath.

He unlocks the top desk drawer and pulls out the cash box. He opens the box and then slams it shut when he sees less cash than he'd hoped for.

It's drastically low. Adrian runs his hands over his face and a groan reverberates through him. He swallows the sickening feeling creeping up his throat and locks the drawer. His eyes sting at the thought of the twenty people counting on him. *We don't have long to go.* He remembers the meeting with the government and laughs at the six weeks waiting period. *We'll be long gone by then.*

He kicks his chair back as he stands, and it falls backwards with a clang. He moves to the door and reefs it open, slamming it close when he steps into the hall.

"Adrian?" Tessa says hesitantly a few feet away. "Are you ok?"

Adrian moves to wave her off but notices his hand tremor. He sucks in a breath and digs his hands into pockets.

He spins away from Tessa. "I'm fine."

The door of Eddy's office opens and Eddy leans out the doorway. "What's going on?"

Adrian rolls his eyes and keeps walking. "Everything's fine."

Eddy steps into the hall and grabs Adrian's arm. "Hey, what is it?"

Adrian stops and nods towards Eddy's office. "You have someone in with you. They need you. Go back in. I'm fine."

Eddy looks at him, knowing he's not fine, but nods. Adrian and Eddy have always agreed the people who come here for shelter and support come first.

"Ok, we'll talk after," Eddy says, returning to his office.

Adrian's hands ball into fists in his pockets as he winds through the hall towards the bedrooms. His jaw clenches, hoping no one stops him with a problem. One more issue and he may explode.

He watches Maria make her way towards the common room, and calls out, "Did you put the food away?"

Maria stops and turns to him. "The what?"

Adrian huffs and turns towards the dining room. "Forget it. I'll do it."

Adrian storms through the dining room and whacks the kitchen door open.

Jazz jumps and yelps by the kitchen bench. She clutches her heart, leaning over. "My goodness, Adrian, you scared the life out of me."

Adrian relaxes his shoulders, blinking at her. "Jazz? What are you doing in here?"

Jazz shakes her shoulders, going back to a bag. "Myra and Taz are catching up on sleep so we all vacated the room." Jazz sighs as she organises vegetables on the bench. "I just needed to keep myself busy, you know. It was wild meeting her."

Adrian moves to the bench. "Did Maria ask you to do this?"

Jazz shakes her head. "No, I haven't seen her. I just came in to see if anyone was around and these things looked like they needed a home. Is that ok?"

Adrian releases a breath, smiling. "Yeah, it's completely fine. Do you know where they go?"

Jazz points to the vegetables. "I was thinking the fridge."

Adrian laughs and takes the bag of kitchen supplies. "You take care of those, I'll put these away."

Jazz moves around the bench to follow him. "Well, show me where they go so I'll know for next time."

"Deciding to stick around for a while?"

Jazz backs off half a step. "Oh, no... I just..." She thinks on her words. "Just in case I have to grab something for Hector, or something."

He smiles at her. "It's ok. I'm glad to have your help."

"I'd like to be more useful."

Adrian stacks a few boxes, and asks, "What else do you want to be doing?"

Jazz sighs and leans against the bench. "I guess I need to know the day-to-day running."

Adrian raises an eyebrow as he swings to face her. "Like a schedule?"

She lights up. "Yes, that would be great!"

Adrian laughs and returns to the shelf. "There's no schedule."

"How can that be?"

"Easily. It's not a business. It's just tending to people when they need it, and leaving them alone when they need it. People are free to come and go as they please. It's a drop-in-centre. No schedule."

Jazz huffs as she loads vegetables into the fridge.

Adrian stands and watches Jazz's frustrated body language. "Is routine important to you? Like a compulsive disorder?"

Jazz grimaces. "You think I'm OCD?"

"A few months ago, a guy living here had it. Eddy explained to me what it was." Adrian raises his hands in defence. "I'm just trying to work you out. You're a very mysterious person, Jazz."

Jazz laughs. "Mysterious? Me?"

"At least I can understand everyone else. Every day, I see the fear, the longing, the desperation, on so many people." Adrian takes a step closer to her. "And then there's you. You walk tall when others slouch or cower. You speak properly where everyone else drops letters or uses slang. Even the way you dress."

Jazz pulls at her t-shirt. "I got this here."

"You just look very put together that's all." He takes a step back, smiling. "I'm not trying to insult you. They are not bad qualities. You're just different."

"Is that why you dress so neatly?" Jazz asks, stepping around him and looking him up and down. "Still a t-shirt and jeans, but no rips, stains or crinkles. Common enough to say you're one of them, but elevated enough to show you're someone of authority who can help."

Adrian splutters a laugh. "Authority?"

Jazz shrugs. "It must feel nice to be in a position of power."

"Hey, hey. I'm not trying to wield power over anyone."

"Something brought you to start up a place like this. Or did you take it over from someone else? Like a family member or mentor?"

"You know, you're very good at deflecting."

"What are you talking about?"

"Any time I ask you about yourself, you turn it back around on me."

"Do you notice that because there's something you are keeping secret? What are you hiding from, Adrian?"

Adrian laughs. "Nice try. At some point you have to talk to someone."

"What makes you think there's anything to talk about?"

"Everyone who stays here has something to talk about."

Jazz smiles. "Does that mean if I don't talk, I should leave?"

Adrian grins, about to joke he needs another kitchenhand, but his smile drops when he remembers his money situation.

Jazz's expression grows serious. "Adrian? What's wrong?"

Adrian shakes his head, forcing a smile as he holds his hips. "No, nothing."

"You've been nothing but a ball of optimism since I got here, and now you look like you've met death. What's the matter?"

Sweat takes over Adrian's forehead. He quickly wipes it off and slips past Jazz. "It's nothing for you to worry about. No one here should have to worry about it, but me."

"Hey," Jazz hushes, clutching his forearm. Adrian stops and looks back at her. "Like you said, everyone needs someone to talk to. You're obviously stressed. What is it?"

When Jazz lets him go, Adrian sighs and his posture collapses. "There's no money."

"What do you mean? Like stolen?"

His eyes widen as he shakes his head. "No, it's just gone. We don't have any donations, and more and more people need help." His eyes wander to the door leading to the back alley. "This city is all kinds of messed up. The rich have everything and everyone else has to struggle for food or shelter." He sighs and turns his back to her as his face creases. "It's not fair."

"I had no... I didn't..." Jazz pauses, and Adrian feels her hand squeeze his shoulder. "I'm sorry. But you shouldn't feel you have to take on all the burden."

Adrian turns to her. "But everyone relies on me."

"Sure, you support everyone, especially on an emotional level. I've watched you tend to every person here like they are the only one here. But they all lend a hand. No way are they expecting you to be solely in charge of the money coming in. I'm sure if you asked people like Hector and Maria, they would help with fundraising ideas."

"I just don't want to put that pressure on them. They do enough lending their time." His face grows pale as he chews his lip. "I shouldn't have let Myra and Taz in this morning, but I couldn't turn them away."

"Of course not. You talk to Eddy about this stuff?"

Adrian nods. "He knows."

Jazz takes a deep breath, and then says, "I can help you find ways to get money."

"Really?"

"I have business training." Jazz purses her lips, looking hesitant, so Adrian decides to not ask her to elaborate. "If you're comfortable showing me your expense figures and where you already have funds coming from, I can work out an action plan."

"Are you sure?"

Jazz nods, smiling. "It'd make me feel useful."

Adrian smiles. "Well, if it'd help you feel better, I'll gladly take your help." They keep eye contact, smiling, as tingles play at Adrian's limbs. He lowers the tension and teases her with, "Lord knows your kitchen game is a little off."

Jazz scoffs, unable to hide her grin. "Is that so?"

Adrian's smile grows to the point his cheeks hurt. "It's a little funny watching you. You make the most mundane tasks look so hard."

"Oh, stop it."

"Who knew dusting needed so many instructions?"

"That's it," Jazz says, fully letting her guard down and lunging towards the sink and flicking sudsy water at him.

Adrian blocks the attack. "Hey, settle down. See, you don't even know what to do with washing up water."

Jazz laughs and splashes him again.

"Be careful, I may attack back."

Jazz lifts her hands, water running down her arms.

"Thanks," Adrian says, reaching for a towel, but then swiftly scoops a hand into the water and splashes Jazz.

Jazz shrieks, her hands flailing in front of her face. "Ok, truce. Truce!"

Adrian laughs, drying his hands. "Truce."

Jazz swipes the towel from him to dry her hands and arms.

Adrian rolls his shoulders back and feels a weight lifted after unburdening to Jazz. He fixates on the shine of her hair as it falls by her face and the magnetism of her dark almond eyes. A tingle runs down his spine as he thinks she's just as beautiful as the first moment he saw her.

"Thank you for offering to help," he says. "I appreciate it and I'd like to hear your ideas to keep this place afloat."

"You do such good for many people. Maiden City needs this place." Jazz smiles and rubs his arm. "We need you here, happy and well."

Adrian swallows awkwardly, blushing from the soft pressure of her hand.

Jazz lowers her gaze, taking her hand away. "I might go check on

Myra and Taz."

Adrian steps aside. "Ok, sounds good."

Spoilt

Jazz tussles her hair in front of the mirror, a smile tingling her lips. She plays with how the waves fall, and curls a lock by her ear, enjoying the moment of feeling feminine. The moment is for her. Not to gain maximum engagement on a Collage post.

She giggles at her reflection. Her heart warms with the thought that she doesn't mind if Adrian notices how she looks.

"You look pretty," Myra says, fixing the shawl around her hairline.

Jazz blushes. "Thanks. The colours of the pashmina really suit your complexion."

"Brings out the bruises?" Myra smirks.

"I hardly notice them."

"You're a bad liar."

"Sorry." Jazz looks down at the lilac sun dress she took from the donation pile. "Does this look all right?"

"Yes, perfect."

Jazz felt bad taking another item of clothing from the donations, but she couldn't handle wearing the same outfit after her shower. She plans to donate a good portion of her wardrobe once she returns home.

"Do you want to go to the common room?"

Myra winces. "Bit noisy."

"I can try to find some games or something for Taz and bring them back."

"That'd be nice. Thank you."

"My pleasure."

Jazz makes her way to the common room where the sounds of teenage boys hits her before seeing them. She shrieks as a billiards ball flies her direction and smacks the wall behind her.

"Shit! Sorry," DJ calls out.

Jazz slams a hand over her racing heart. "Sorry? That could have hit me in the face."

"It was my fault," Ferg says, sliding in front of DJ with arms out wide. "I was teasing him and he hit the ball wrong."

Jazz lowers her hand and composes herself walking towards the boys. "You guys have made up?"

Max slides an arm over DJ's shoulder. "We're all besties."

Jazz eyes DJ. "All good?"

"Seriously, we are all good." DJ smirks and adds, "Sorry for almost destroying your pretty face."

Jazz flinches from the dryness of his words. "Ok?" She looks between the boys; wary things may not be well despite their words. "Apology accepted."

Ferg runs a hand over his cropped auburn hair, puffing out his chest. "Is there anything we can do for you, Miss?"

Jazz peers around the room. "I saw a box of children's toys in here somewhere. Where was that?"

Max points beside the couch. "Over there."

Jazz spots the crate. "Ah, thank you." She lifts it up and spins to the doorway. "Thanks, boys."

"See, she's not that uptight," Ferg stage-whispers to the boys.

"Heard that," Jazz teases, leaving the room to the sounds of nervous laughter.

She missed arm day at the gym but carrying this box back to the room makes up for it.

"Here we are," Jazz says, entering the bedroom. She kneels to the floor as Taz runs towards her. "See all this cool stuff, little man."

"Wow," Taz says, extending the o.

Jazz giggles, helping him take out the toys. "I know, how fun."

"Thanks, Jazz," Myra says through gritted teeth as she pulls herself further up the bed.

"Myra?" Jazz moves towards the bed. "Are you ok?"

"My side is killing me."

Jazz places her hand over Myra's which digs into her ribs. "Perhaps we should take you to the hospital."

"No way. He'll be looking for me there."

"It'll be safe."

"*No*," Myra snaps. "You don't understand what it's like for someone like me."

Jazz leans back from the bed. "I'm sorry."

Myra purses her lips, her eyes steely on her son. "I didn't mean to yell, but have you ever been to The Limits? You probably live in a palace, right?"

"I'm here now," Jazz whispers. "Why don't you educate me?"

Myra *tsks*, rolling her eyes. "Like you want to know."

Jazz moves closer to the bed, clasping Myra's hand. "I do. Tell me. Tell me about your life."

Myra locks eyes with Jazz. Her eyes droop with sorrow. "It wasn't always like this." Jazz squeezes her hand, letting her continue. "I had a good childhood. Good parents. Great brothers. Nice people at the mosque. But then teenage rebellion happened..." Myra's lip upturns at the memory. "It was so silly. I wanted to be like the blonde girls in the magazines. And then I met Danny."

"Taz's father?"

Myra nods, a disgusted expression crossing her face. "The worst mistake. I found him dangerous, mysterious, handsome, and romantic."

Dangerous and romantic?

"You're probably judging me hard."

Jazz sucks in a breath, and her eyes widen. "No, not at all."

Myra grins. "Bad liar."

Jazz winces. "Sorry."

Myra bats her free hand. "Don't worry about it. It was just foolish sixteen-year-old thoughts. We had a good year, but then he started hitting me." Tears form in the corners of her eyes. "I tried to leave, but he'd stop me or find me before I reached my parents." She swallows hard. "Then I became pregnant, and he said I couldn't leave."

Jazz interlocks their fingers, willing herself not to cry.

Myra whispers, "It wasn't with Taz." Tears roll down her face. "I had a miscarriage because he'd still hit me. I lost my first baby because of him."

Jazz rushes her body over Myra's. She hovers over her, careful not to hurt her wound, and strokes the shawl over her hair while keeping herself close.

Myra presses her hands into Jazz's back. "The last three years have been a living hell."

"I won't let him hurt you again," Jazz whispers. "I promise."

"Mummy," Taz's small voice pipes up.

Jazz lifts herself from Myra, who wipes her face and smiles at her son. "Yeah baby?"

Taz pouts, looking between the two women.

Jazz wipes her face dry and smiles at Taz. "We're ok, little man. Did you find something fun in the box?"

Taz grins, lifting two toy trucks.

Jazz gasps with enthusiasm. "Wow, that's awesome."

Taz shows them how to push the trucks along the carpet and Jazz applauds him. She eyes Myra, who slumps to the side, watching her son.

"I'll get you a doctor," Jazz whispers.

Myra searches Jazz's face. "What?"

"I'll bring a doctor here. A good one. You know I have the means."

Myra smiles. "Thank you. But play with Taz first, I might take a nap."

"Ok," Jazz whispers and moves closer to Taz. "Can I have a go?"

Taz slides a truck over and Jazz pushes the truck back and forth. "Like this?"

Taz takes the truck back and shows her how to push the truck forward only.

"Oh, was I not doing it correctly?" Jazz asks with a laugh.

Jazz eyes Myra lying on the bed and she finds it difficult to keep her face happy for Taz's benefit. Her stomach churns, and revulsion at her own privileged life seeps through her body.

Taz yawns, and Jazz helps him onto the bed to curl up against his mother. She closes the door on the two after blowing him a kiss.

She leans against the wall as guilt weighs her down. *How could I ever think I've been so mistreated?* She grits her teeth as her eyes slit and sting. *I am a spoilt brat.*

Proud

Jazz lands at Eddy's office and knocks on the door. After a few moments, footsteps sound closer from inside.

The door opens, and Eddy pops his head out. "Jazz, everything ok? I'm just in a session with someone at the moment."

"I don't have any real problems," Jazz blurts out, her arms flailing at her sides. "I don't know what I'm doing with my life."

Eddy takes her hands and clasps them in front of her. He locks eyes with her. "Just breathe." He demonstrates a slow breath in and out. "Breathe."

Jazz inhales and exhales in time with Eddy.

Eddy squeezes her hands and nods to a seat by the door. "Take a seat. We won't be long."

"Ok," Jazz whispers and sits down, feeling as fragile as glass.

Eddy returns inside, closing the door. Jazz listens to the murmurs of the conversation inside but doesn't pick up any of the words. She rubs her heart and bats her eyes dry.

After a few minutes, the door opens and Ferg walks into the hall, his head down to not meet Jazz's gaze. He waves a hand behind him, saying, "Thanks, Eddy," as he continues down the hall.

"No problem," Eddy says, stopping in the doorway. He looks to Jazz. "You want to come in?"

Jazz slouches. "I'm sorry, I shouldn't have interrupted like that."

"No, it's fine."

"It was rude. And you probably have something scheduled for now." Jazz rushes off the seat and backs down the hall. "Sorry, I shouldn't have presumed I could just come here."

Eddy steps into the hall, beckoning her closer. "I told you my door is always open." He smiles to himself. "Well, not literally, but you can always stop by. Now, c'mon. Come inside."

Jazz sighs and nods, following Eddy into his office. He shows her to a couch, and she perches on the edge.

"You can relax," Eddy says, leaning against his desk. "Are you nervous?"

Jazz anchors her elbows on her knees and collapses her face in her hands. "I shouldn't have any right to feel cheated."

"What makes you say that?"

Jazz lifts her head, sliding back on the couch. "I come from a privileged background and I've complained about things not going my way my whole life. What gives me the right when people like Myra have suffered so much?"

Eddy gently pushes his palms out. "Slow down. You're allowed to have feelings and have things upset you. Your emotions are valid."

"They come from a place of being spoilt." Jazz huffs at the carpet. "It's like I'm seeing myself for the first time."

"You can't put yourself down. You can only have the experiences life throws at you. How can you know lives like this exist if you've never encountered them before?"

Jazz meets Eddy's eyes, and she ponders the thought. "I guess that's true."

Eddy sits on the desk and his thin lips create the warmest smile as the green of his eyes play against the sunlight.

"Something about you is very comforting."

Eddy lets out a breathy laugh. "Thanks. I should be honest and say I'm aware you're Darius Abadi's daughter."

Jazz sucks in a breath, her back snapping rigid.

He lifts a hand. "It's ok. If you're running from something you're allowed to be here, just as much as anyone else."

"It's all confidential in here, right?"

"Of course."

She relaxes her posture. "Ok."

"I've been to one of your gyms. *Swanky*."

A limp smile curls her lips. "Thanks, we try."

"It was just too upmarket for me, so I had to leave. Sorry."

Jazz shrugs. "If you weren't comfortable." She can't help looking around the shabby office.

"It was while I was studying at university," Eddy points out. "I live in Province and so it was close by."

Jazz feels her demeanour change around him, her uptight, professional service persona wanting to take over, because he's 'one of us.'

"You're from Province?"

"It's the only part of Maiden City my parents deem appropriate to live. Apart from Sovereign Hill, that is."

Jazz bites her lip. "I'm from Sovereign Hill. What do your parents do?"

"They're doctors. They've always worked around the clock. I was on track to be like them, but I wanted to slow down so I could focus more deeply on my patients. Then came this place." Eddy rests his hands on his knees and asks, "What is it like with your parents?"

Jazz's arms curve around her mid-section, her body closing in.

"Oh, I'm sorry," Eddy blurts. "Your mother. I'm sorry, I know from the media your mother's no longer with us." He clears his throat. "My condolences."

Jazz tilts her head to the side, face stony. "It was a long time ago."

"Doesn't make it any less of a loss."

Jazz turns to Eddy, her eyes weakened by tears. "It was my fault."

Eddy's gaze intensifies, his chin dipping as he waits for her to continue.

"If I never existed, she'd still be alive."

"Your existence didn't kill your mother."

"She died giving birth to me."

"You can't blame yourself. Have you always felt this way?"

Jazz swallows dryly and nods.

Eddy moves to a chair, leaning towards her. "Did your father put the blame on you?"

"We don't talk about her."

"Recently? Or did he never tell you stories about her?"

"I know she was a jazz musician, that's where I got my name, and I know she was excited to be a mother..." Jazz frowns at the dismal memories. "But that's about it."

"Have you asked your father to share more about her?"

"Not since I was young." Jazz hugs herself tight, picturing her father's face. "He always looked so pained when thinking about her. I didn't want to keep making him sad. I didn't want him to blame me. Outright blame me for her being gone. I didn't want him to connect the dots... but I know he already has."

"You're putting too much pressure and guilt on yourself." Eddy pauses, waiting for her to meet his eyes. "Your father has never said the words, 'it's your fault,' has he?"

Her shoulders droop as she tugs on her knees. "No."

"What makes you think it's acceptable to live your life with that burden? What would you say to someone else who told you they were living this way?"

"I'm not an unfortunate case like other people. I still get to live my life."

"But are you?" Eddy counters. "You came in here saying you don't know what you're doing with your life. What makes you feel incomplete?"

"Incomplete?" Jazz pauses on the thought. She's never investigated that missing piece, always covering it with work, hoping it would fill the void. "Myra must have gotten me thinking about it. In another life she could have been me. And her sweet baby boy. He just awoke something in me. Something I never let out."

"Tell me more about that side of you."

Jazz sighs, resting against the couch. "Maybe because I never had a mother, I wanted to protect myself against the idea of children." She bites her lip and plays with a lock of hair. "I want to make my father proud. I want to be part of the company and be worthy in his eyes. But that means playing the game like a man. No emotions. Just business."

Eddy clasps his hands over his face as he blows out a laboured breath. "Wow, there's so much to unpack there." Jazz winces at his reaction and he's quick to add, "You're not wrong. There's no right or wrong in how we navigate life. It's about what we learn."

"So, what should I learn?"

"That's for you to work out. Is business the only thing you and your father bond over?"

"Bond?"

"Do you have any other things you discuss? What about jazz music? Do you ever sit down and listen to it together? To remember your mother?"

Jazz cuts her breath short. Her eyes fog. "As a little girl, I played one of her recordings, and my father stopped the music and took it away."

"Oh Jazz." He leans over and touches her knee. "I'm so sorry."

Her voice breaks, "He took her away."

"Is that when you stopped asking about your mother?"

Jazz sniffs, wiping her eyes and nodding.

"Here," Eddy says, offering a box of tissues.

"Thank you," she whispers, pulling three tissues.

"You want to get close to your father through the family business?"

"My father is a very important man and many people seek his advice. He fought for his place in this city. He worked his way up in a society that initially didn't accept him, and his success is to my advantage." She swipes a tissue under her eye. "The only way I know how to talk to my father is through the company. I want him to be proud of me and be happy I'm alive."

"And you feel you can't be your real self to do that?"

Jazz tilts her head, mouth dropping open as she lowers the tissue.

"You said you have to work with no emotions and play the game like a man," Eddy reminds. "Side-stepping the offence that men don't have emotions, the more important takeaway is that you feel you can't be your true self to make your father proud."

Jazz utters the beginning of words, trying to form a response, until, "Perhaps it was easier?"

"Do you want to run the company?"

"I think so."

"Not sure?"

"I used to be."

"And being here changed that?"

Jazz looks to the ceiling but can't deny her answer. She looks to Eddy, finding herself smiling. "Yes."

Eddy smiles back. "And you're happy about that?"

Her smile grows. "Yes."

"Would you like adding thoughts of your mother back into your life?"

"Yes, but I wouldn't know where to start."

"You enjoyed interacting with Taz. Does being around children remind you of her?"

"I was told she was a very compassionate person and had very fine-tuned maternal instincts."

"Something you hid from yourself?"

"It was too hard recognising parts of her in me."

"But you're ready to change that?"

Jazz puffs out a breath. "Definitely."

"Then perhaps volunteer work is an avenue you can take to honour your mother's memory? You like being a part of this place?"

Jazz nods, and then her eyes round. "But it's almost out of money. I can fix that. I can help."

"Adrian would appreciate it."

"I told him I would help." Jazz looks at Eddy sceptically. "Does he know my last name? Who I am?"

"Adrian doesn't follow the upper-class world. He has some issues with the class system. He's never even seen a Collage page."

"Oh my," Jazz hushes. "We are truly from different worlds."

"All the more ways you can help each other."

"Oh, Eddy, thank you so much for talking this through with me." She stands with an unsure expression on her face. "Can I hug you?"

Eddy lets out a breathy laugh and stands with his arm stretched out. "Sure."

Jazz wraps him in a hug. "Thank you. Thank you."

He pats her back. "My pleasure."

"Do you have a phone? I need to call a doctor."

Brave

"**Gene**, when did you get so good at this?" Holly asks as Gene gathers her silky blonde hair from behind her.

Gene smirks. "Would it be weird to say I practiced on dolls?"

Holly laughs. "Yes, but if you can actually make me look like a movie star, I don't care."

"I'm just glad for a real-life model," Gene says, twisting parts of Holly's hair into each other.

Holly giggles, playing with her necklace. "You think I'm a model?"

Gene's eyebrows raise at her dumbness but goes with it. "Sure Holly. You're the most beautiful girl in school." He wasn't lying. Holly was the *it girl* of Walsh High School.

"What are you doing with your hands all over my girlfriend, freak?" Rhett sneers, looming over the pair, puffing his chest.

"Calm down," Holly says, waving him off. "Gene's just doing my hair."

"What are you, some kind of fairy?" Rhett says, loud enough for the entire schoolyard to hear. He laughs boisterously, holding his belly.

Gene's back knots as Rhett's friends gather, laughing and pointing at him.

"C'mon, Nancy," Rhett says, stepping forward and shoving Gene. "You a little faggot, or what?"

"Rhett!" Holly snaps. "Leave him alone."

Gene regains his balance, dodging Rhett's next shove.

One of Rhett's friends laughs, saying, "*Aw*, the fag don't wanna dance with ya, Rhett."

Rhett shoves Gene again, and Gene groans, pushing Rhett back and yelling, "Fine! Yes, I am."

Rhett smirks. "*Ha*, what? You're admitting it, you little queer?"

"Yes, I'm queer," Gene replies. He leaps up on the bench, spreading his arms out wide. "Walsh High School, I'm Gene Williams and I'm gay!"

"*Woo!*" Holly cheers, clapping and smiling by Gene's feet.

Rhett points to Holly. "You're applauding this shit?"

"Of course." She points to her hair. "D'you see what he created up here. He's a genius."

"With hair?" Rhett teases.

Gene leaps off the bench and lands in front of Rhett. "Yes, with hair." He keeps his arms out wide, standing on tiptoes to reach Rhett's height. "What of it? I'm gonna be a stylist."

Rhett raises an eyebrow, looking back at his friends who are speechless, answering in shrugs.

Gene locks eyes with Rhett, waiting for the next hateful remark.

Rhett ignores Gene and looks to Holly. "You've got a lot to think about if you're siding with this poof instead of me."

Gene's heart pounds in his chest. *And a fifth colourful term.* Rhett and his friends turn and walk away, and Gene feels his blood slow in his veins. *Phew, no busted-in nose.*

Holly jumps up and loops her arm around Gene's and tussles his dark brown hair which swirls in waves atop his head. "Congratulations. You were so brave to come out."

Holly's friends circle them, throwing congratulations laced with giggles.

Gene pulls Holly closer. "You can do better than that loser."

Holly rolls her eyes. "Not in this high school."

That's just dumb. Gene gestures to the bench. "C'mon, lemme finish your hair."

Holly squeals as she sits. "Girls, do I look like a movie star, or what?"

As the girls agree with Holly and ask Gene if they can be next, his mind wanders to home. He came out at school. Could he be that courageous in front of his parents?

On the walk home from school, he practises his lines to his parents. He passes the small family homes lined by the sidewalk. Hamlet is the working-class area of Maiden City. His parents, and the parents of his classmates, work for the upper class that runs the city. Hamlet is nowhere near as bad as The Limits, but Gene knows in his heart he wants to get out of here one day.

"Oi, faggot!" Rhett's voice booms behind him.

Are you serious? Gene groans as goosebumps sprout on his arms. He slows his pace and turns to see Rhett and two of his friends pacing towards him.

"Look, he responded to it," Rhett's right-side goon teases.

"No one makes me out for a fool," Rhett grizzles, picking up Gene by the collar. "Especially in front of my girlfriend."

Gene chokes, squinting as Rhett's breath blows on his face. "Didn't know you wanted to get so close," Gene croaks.

Rhett tosses Gene backwards. "*Ehck*! You pile of pus." Rhett moves in quick with a swift kick to Gene's stomach.

Gene curls inward, coughing in pain as his stomach contorts.

Rhett's friends laugh, cheering him on. Rhett kicks Gene again and then pulls him up to standing. "Don't let me see you again," he says in a mean whisper, and punches Gene below the eye.

As Gene hits the cracked cement, the boys jog away. Their footsteps sending pounding into Gene's ears, strengthening the radiating pain in his face. Gene pushes his palm into his cheek and the pain sears into his forehead. He takes his hand away and somehow, it's more painful.

After a few minutes, Gene picks himself up from the sidewalk and ambles his way home.

Gene's insides churn as he walks through the front door.

His mother wanders out of the kitchen. "Hi sweetie, how was school?"

Gene dumps his bag by the front door and keeps his gaze low as he walks further into the house. "It was fine. How was your day?"

"Nothing special." She walks close to him and tilts her head to find his eyes. "Gene, what's wrong?"

"Nothing."

She grabs his chin and lifts his face. She gasps at the shine on his cheek. "Is that a bruise? What happened?"

Gene reefs his head back, and a headache splits his vision. "It's nothing."

His father stands from his armchair, tossing his book on the side table. "What's this nonsense, Gene?"

Gene groans. "It's not nonsense."

"Sweetie, just tell us what happened."

Gene shrugs. "Some guys jumped me."

His father moves in front of him, crossing his arms. "Did you strike back?"

Gene winces. "Strike back?"

"Yes, defend yourself."

"No. I don't see the point to adding to mindless violence."

His father groans, turning his back on him. "Weak."

"It wouldn't have done any good," Gene argues. "They

outnumbered me.”

“Excuses.”

“They don’t like me. They don’t like me because of who I am.”

His father turns back. “What does that mean? Because you’re my son?”

Gene rolls his eyes. *As if it’d be about you.*

His father grabs him by the collar and lifts him so his feet are off the ground. “Answer me.”

“No, it’s not you. They don’t like me.”

His mother grabs her husband’s wrists. “Let him go. Gene, just tell us what happened.”

Gene wriggles out of his father’s grip and backs away. “They hate me because I’m gay!”

His mother gasps, clasping her open mouth. His father’s face reddens as he threatens, “Take that back.”

“Take what back?”

“You heard me. Take it back. I don’t want such filth spoken in my house.”

“It’s not filth. I’m trying to tell you who I am.”

His mother sniffles. “Oh, Gene, please stop it.”

He looks to his mother, heart breaking. “Stop what?”

“Don’t act stupid!” his father yells. “Now take it back.”

“Dad, I’m gay.”

Crack. His father’s fist connects with Gene’s cheek so quick he didn’t see it coming. The pain inflames behind his eye and drills into the top of his skull. He falls to his knees, clutching his head, his vision spinning and darkening.

“Get up,” his father taunts, his voice menacing.

Gene hunches over his knees, pressing his palm into his face to minimise the pain.

“GET UP.”

“*Gene,*” his mother cries.

Gene presses hard into his face. The pain worsens but is dulled by the adrenaline pumping through his veins. He stands and dashes to the front door, swiping his bag and racing out of the house.

"You get back here, you little bastard!" his dad calls out, but Gene doesn't stop running. He runs faster than he's ever run before. Faster than his thoughts can catch up.

Just run. Just get away. Get to anywhere. Anywhere is better than here.

Panicking

Gene only slows when his feet hurt. The run from Hamlet into the city was far, and he looks around for a place to stay. He grips the straps of his backpack, sure he's not carrying any money with him. He sweats and gulps as the evening darkens the sky.

He moves from street to street until he winds up in the Nightclub District. His pulse thunders in his ears. Scantily dressed women in fishnet stockings and thigh-high boots walk the streets, waiting for cars to pull up. Men with long, neon strips of hair down the middle of their bald heads, cladded in studded leather, exchange bags of pills for cash in the alleys.

He hugs himself and walks close to the buildings, trying to not make eye contact with anyone as he passes.

Two sinister guys, with tattoos along their necks and sides of their heads, look him up and down. Gene quickens his steps and pulls his bag close, turning down an alley.

The men gain on him. Gene runs by a dumpster and turns down the next alley behind a graffitied building. He pants, heart pounding, and dives behind another dumpster. His throat is lit with flames from his panicked breathing. His chest rapidly rises and falls as he concentrates on the footsteps of the two men.

"*Oi.*"

"Ah!" Gene yells in panic.

"*Shoosh*," a girl hushes, leaning over him, placing a finger over her lips. She wears dark sunglasses even though it's night, and she angles her head to watch the other end of the alley. "What are you doing here?"

"Panicking," he whispers, heart about to explode.

She anchors herself between the dumpster and the graffitied brick wall, her khaki bomber jacket ballooning off her thin frame. She rests a heavy, black steel-capped boot on a bag of rubbish and lowers herself to Gene. "Follow me."

Gene gulps and ponders what else he has to lose. He fixes his bag to his back and follows the girl to the end of the alley.

She pulls at a wire fence and nods to him. "In."

Gene grows pale but forces himself through the hole. Wire scrapes his bare forearms. He's tugged backwards and is shaken with panic. His nerves calm when the girl sets his bag free from the wire it snagged on.

"Got any food in that?"

Gene frowns. "No."

"What's the point of carrying it?"

He waits for her to lead, thinking about his most cherished possessions inside his backpack.

"I haven't seen you around," she says, pushing through a line of shrubs.

"I've never been around here." His lip upturns as the leaves brush against his clothes.

"You're too pretty for the streets."

"Come again?"

"You shouldn't be out here. Where did you come from?"

"My home. But I can't go back there."

"Why?"

Gene halts. "Hang on. Why should I spill my guts? What's your story?"

She keeps walking.

"Hey, I asked you a question."

"You want somewhere to sleep, or not?"

Gene groans and hurries to catch up.

The girl swings herself onto fire-escape stairs, and Gene stares at the rust and imagines her falling through a broken stair.

"You coming?" she calls out.

Gene inhales deeply and pulls himself up onto the first rung. He steps behind her and asks what her name is.

"What do you want to know for?"

Gene *tsks*. "Are you always so on guard? I'm Gene."

"Gene?" She snorts. Sarcasm thick in her tone. "Your parents must love you."

"Well, not really, actually. You happy now?"

She stops and looks over her shoulder at him, dark shades covering her eyes but her frown clearly visible. "I'm sorry. I don't have parents either."

"Well, don't get me wrong, they're alive and all, they just..." He shakes his head and gestures to his bruised face. "It's complicated. Bad enough to not go back."

She turns back and jogs up the next few steps.

"How long have you been living out here?"

"I started younger than you are."

"I could be twenty-five."

She snorts. "Nice try. I'm twenty-five. You look twelve."

"Oh, c'mon. I'm fifteen." He raises an eyebrow. "Are you saying you've been on the streets since before you were twelve?"

She ducks into an open window, dodging the question. Gene takes the hint she won't talk about herself and chucks a leg over the windowsill and pushes himself inside.

"*Oof.* What is that?" Gene retches, slamming his palm over his mouth while pinching his nose. His eyes water and stomach churns from a pungent, grotesque smell he doesn't have the capacity to describe. *There's something dead in here.*

"Keep moving," she orders, stomping through open and torn bags of rubbish.

Gene gags as he moves through rotten food and piles of old belongings left to decay. "Why did you bring me here?"

"It's safe."

"Safe? Not from disease."

She spins around, blonde hair whipping around her head as her hands grip around Gene's throat. He gasps for air as her fingernails dig into his throat.

She moves her face as close to his as possible. The breath from her nostrils puff into Gene's mouth as he strains for air. Sweating, he stares at his fearful expression in the reflection of her dark shades.

"You want me to throw you out the window?" she whispers. Crunches sound below their feet as she forces him backwards in one step. "Huh? Rather try your luck outside with the junkies and the gangbangers?"

Gene squeaks mid-gulp and shakes his head. His eyes are moments from popping out.

She releases him, and he drops to his knees, gasping to refill his lungs. His hands press into the floor and even though he's clutching sticky and wet things in the muck, he doesn't care. Adrenaline shakes his body as a voice in his head tells him to get up.

"You coming?" she asks, walking away from him.

He lifts his head and swallows what feels like broken glass. He eyes her boots and his fists curl as anger lights in his chest. "Who are you?"

She keeps walking.

"Hey!" he yells. "Tell me who you are!"

She stops but doesn't turn around. "Get your arse up."

He groans, hurting his throat further, and pulls himself up. He wipes his palms over his pants and immediately regrets the decision. He picks up his backpack and flings it over his shoulders.

He catches up to her. "I think I deserve to know your name."

She huffs a response.

"Are you helping me, or getting ready to kill me?"

"If you don't shut up, I will lead you to your death." She crouches and pushes on a section of the wall and opens a hatch. "In ya get."

Gene backs up. "Oh, hell no." Every horror movie he'd ever seen flashes in a montage in his mind.

She dips her glasses, showing the top of her eyes, and whispers, "Get in."

Something strangely calming rushes over Gene, and he crouches down beside her and crawls into the space.

He sits with bent knees and finds he can't stretch any further.

"I'll come back for you in the morning," she says, closing the hatch.

"What? No!" he yells, kicking the faux door.

She pulls the covering back and *tsks*. "Calm down. I'm not going far. Now *shoosh* before you tell the whole planet about my hidey-hole."

Gene's heart bashes against his ribs and the sweat is slick down the sides of his face. "Don't leave me."

She puts a finger to her lips and then draws a cross over heart. She closes the hatch and leaves Gene in darkness with the sounds of his breathing and her disappearing footsteps.

Help

Jazz tightens the laces of the size too big, running shoes she found in the donations. She put the Baby tee back on and found shorts that are a size too small. The elastic of the shorts digs into her stomach as she runs. But she's grateful. Grateful to be moving again.

The guilt of not checking in with her gym has weighed on her, but she knows they will be fine. There is a contingency plan for her absence. She has stepped away at the last minute many times in the past. Any time her father asks her to join him at a corporate retreat or a conference out of the city. Marcus will manage just fine in her absence.

She stops. *Marcus?* She dismissed him. He had been her second in charge. Jazz huffs and picks up her pace. *Whatever, they'll have figured it out.*

Her ponytail swishes against her back as she runs, bypassing the Nightclub District. As she runs the streets grow grittier, the graffiti more prominent, and the buildings more dilapidated. The windows are broken, boarded, or barred. Jazz slows her pace, panning the neighbourhood. Her hand rests on her hastening heart. Her breathing is shallow as her mouth hangs open. *People live like this?*

She picks up her pace as residents move in and out of buildings.

Myra accused her of not knowing what it's like in The Limits and it has played on her mind. She needed to experience it, to see it, not to be told about it from the perspective of upper class eyes.

She never thought it was actually this bad. It's not fair. If everyone from Sovereign Hill shared a small portion of their fortune, they could restore this place and give the people here a real chance at education, employment, and happiness.

When Jazz returns to shelter she goes to the bedroom to get ready for a shower. Myra and Taz's bed is empty even though it's so early. They are not in the bathroom when Jazz takes her shower so expects to see them in the common room or dining room once she's ready.

As the water runs over her head and down her hair to her back, Jazz lets the images of The Limits replay in her mind. She can't remember the last time she reflected so deeply on something that didn't have a money-making angle behind it, or data to import into a spreadsheet. Her concern is the people, not figures. If she can use her finance skills to help them, she will. But she wants to connect. She wants to learn about them and help them find themselves. This is the first time she feels real, like her identity is finally revealed after years of suffocation.

Adrian's smiling face appears in her mind, and her smile pushes at her cheeks. *I need to thank him for sharing this world with me.* He taught her to be empathetic when interacting with people, to slow down and pay attention, and she is grateful. Skills she never thought were important before. She used to treat all her clients the same way, like ticking off a checklist. Now she allows herself to connect on a deeper level. To show true emotions and be present.

Jazz fans her face. *Control yourself.* She got a notepad and pen from Maria last night, and jots down another idea to keep the shelter afloat. She now has quite a list, and she is excited to share them with Adrian. Hopefully, somewhere, just the two of them.

Follow

Gene screams as the hatch rips open and sunlight streams into his tiny cave.

"Calm down," she whispers, crouching by the opening. She holds out her hand. "C'mon."

"You didn't come back," Gene says, shaking uncontrollably.

"I know. I'm sorry."

He grabs her hand. "Get me out of here."

"I wanted you to be safe."

Gene whips his hands from hers. "You need help!"

"Stop yelling."

"Psychological help." He pants, catching his breath. "What kind of twisted person locks someone in a wall cavity?"

"You weren't locked in. You could have gotten out if you really wanted. How do you think I use it?"

Gene slides his phone into his backpack, and notices how crusty and raw his eyes feel. His phone has ten percent battery left. He used it all night as a light and didn't sleep a wink. Instead, he sat terrified, hearing every small creak and loud bang.

"Let's go," she says, moving towards the window they came in.

Gene doesn't move. "Tell me where."

"I'm dropping you off."

"You are giving me to a gang to be murdered?"

She laughs, lifting a leg out the window. "I wouldn't have wasted the entire night if it were that easy."

Gene grumbles and makes his way to the window. He thought he'd be used to the smell by now, but nope.

In the morning sun the stairs look more dangerous, but he rushes down to follow the troubling girl.

"Hurry up," she calls out, not looking back as her heavy black boots stomp against the cement.

Gene wonders why he's following her. She still hasn't revealed her name or why she wanted to 'help him.' He's sceptical of her help. He made it through the night, but, inside the wall cavity, he bruised his shoulders every time an unnerving sound from outside made him flinch or jump.

Gene catches up to the girl as she leads him out of the Nightclub District.

She points to a building at the end of an alley. "The guy in there will help you."

Gene steps ahead of her and sees a guy with soft brunette hair and open body language. "Why? Who is he?"

When she doesn't reply, Gene turns around. "Oh c'mon," he whines, throwing his hands up when she's nowhere in sight.

Gene digs his hands into his pockets as he looks back to the alley. The handsome guy, with the good hair, is talking to two people. His arms are folded and he is looking down. Sad. The people talking to him nod and turn away.

Handsome guy seems embarrassed or guilty. Gene dawdles his way down the alley, and passes the couple as one says, "He said we could try the church."

Gene frowns. *He's turning people away.* He stops in place and takes in the features of the alleyway. It's a cleaner alley than he's seen in the last twelve hours, but still a dump. *This place is supposed to help me?*

The guy stops by the door and stares at Gene. Gene bites his lip and his fingers curl in his pockets, willing him to say hi. The guy's head tilts and his eyes squint. Gene angles his head, realising he'd be taking in the bruises on his face.

The guy's lips curl in a delicate smile. He waves and says, "You hungry?"

Gene's heart rapid beats against his ribs. He clasps his hands together and steps forward. "You sure?"

The guy's smile widens, and it's like the sun appears for a second time. He beckons Gene closer. "C'mon. I need some breakfast myself."

"Thanks. I didn't know where to go." Gene walks to the guy, looking over his shoulder for the psychotic girl. "Someone suggested here."

The guy cranes his neck to see past the alley. "Someone was with you? Do they need help?"

"Tons," Gene blurts. "But I doubt she's willing to take it."

The guy keeps his eyes focused on the street beyond the alley. "Tell me if you see her again."

Gene shrugs. "Sure."

"I'm Adrian," he says, extending his hand. "What's your name?"

"I'm Gene." Gene winces at his hand. "I don't know if you wanna shake my hand. I spent the night in filth."

Adrian takes Gene's hand. "I've seen worse."

Gene jitters. A sensation buzzes inside him, like Adrian is the person who's been missing from his life. He takes in the angles of his face and plans to find a way he can stay around him.

When their hands let go, Gene sucks in a breath and says, "And I'm gay." He's determined to never keep it a secret again.

Adrian waits for him to add more. "Ok."

Gene's eyebrows lift. "It's ok?"

Adrian smiles. "Yeah, of course it's ok. It doesn't matter who you are, as long as you're true to yourself."

Gene's mouth drops open. Adrian squints at him and Gene shakes out of it, saying, "Sorry, it's just not the reaction I got at home."

Adrian places a hand on Gene's back. "Come into the dining room. You wanna talk it out?"

Gene blows out a breath as he and Adrian step into the building. "Maybe that'd be good. I can't go home, and I sure as hell ain't going back on the streets. Those gang members scared the crap out of me."

"Neons or the hoods?"

Gene's face screws up. "They had coloured spiky hair. What are the hoods?"

"Just another gang. They wear hooded clothing or cloaks. Both are bad as each other," Adrian explains. "It's getting outta control out there. I'm glad you're off the streets."

Adrian leads the way to the dining room, and Gene's eyes widen at the crowd of people sitting around the long-stretched plastic tables.

"Who are all these people?" Gene whispers as Adrian shows him to the food.

"Just people who need food and shelter." Adrian tilts his head. "Like you."

Gene chews his lip as he pans over the faces at the table. *Like me?*

"Adrian," a female voice calls out. Gene turns around as she asks, "Have you seen Myra and Taz?"

Gene gasps, chin ready to drop to the floor. Her silky raven hair, her glowing olive skin, and toned fitness-pro physique. "You're Jazz Abadi," he announces loud enough for all the heads in the room to turn in his direction.

Jazz's mouth juts open and close as she looks side-to-side, waving her hands to signal a mistake. "What? No, you're mistaking me for someone."

"Jazz?" Adrian questions.

Jazz looks up to the ceiling, wincing.

"It is you," Gene says, stepping towards her, hands clasped. "I love you. I follow everything you do."

Jazz looks over his shoulder to Adrian with pleading eyes.

"How do you know each other?" Adrian asks.

Jazz's eyes droop, but Gene is too excited to notice. He spins to Adrian. "She's Jazz Abadi. *Hello*. Who doesn't know her?"

"*Stop*," Jazz pleads, stomping behind him.

Gene spins to her. "What?"

Jazz doesn't answer and instead turns and races out of the dining room.

Gene turns back to Adrian, who has confusion written all over his face.

"How do you know her?" Adrian asks in a low tone.

Gene mutters nonsensical words. *What? How can he ask that? Everyone follows Jazz Abadi.*

Hiding

Jazz's hands shake over the bathroom basin. She stomps her foot, frowning at her reflection. She has been kidding herself that no one would recognise her and blurt it out in front of the entire shelter. She has a high public profile. It surprises her it has lasted this long.

She clenches her jaw, turning on the cold water. *I hope this doesn't get out and Ethan finds me. If he found this place, he'd probably destroy it just to spite me. The Mayor wants to close down The Limits. Ethan would tell him to start here. I can't let that happen.*

She splashes cold water over her face and inhales deeply. She needs to find Adrian and apologise for not being forthright with him.

Oof! Jazz leaves the bathroom and thwacks into someone. She smooths down her clothes and pulls back her hair to see the wide eyes of the boy that exposed her.

"Oh, hi," she says flatly.

"I'm sorry," he rushes, waving his hands madly. "I'm just such a huge fan. I didn't know you were undercover or something. But that's crazy. How does no one know who you are?"

"Some do," Jazz replies. "They just don't have big mouths."

The boy grows pale. "I'm sorry," he squeaks. He pulls out his phone and opens his Collage account and scrolls through Jazz's feed. "I watch everything you do." The screen goes black. "Crap, it's dead."

Jazz grabs his shoulder and spins him around. "There's a charger in the common room."

"Oh ok," he says, letting Jazz push him along. "I'm Gene, by the way. I'm gay."

"You say that like it's your occupation."

"I'm just not hiding anymore."

Jazz lets him go, pats his back, and smiles. "Well, that's good, Gene. You shouldn't hide who you are."

"So, why are you?" He sucks in a breath when Jazz glares at him. "I'm sorry. It's just I was wondering why your feed went silent. It's so unlike you."

"I'm just taking a break. Everyone needs a break, right?"

"Sure. I just would have thought you would announce a hiatus, not disappear. Did you plan to volunteer here? And what about the company restructure?"

Jazz sighs, sick of his questions. She pushes him down the hall, past the boys' bedrooms, and shoves him into the common room. "You'll find the charger in here." She nods at Ferg and Max. "You can hang with these boys."

Gene stammers words to continue their conversation, but Jazz is quick down the hall. She shakes out her hair, thrown off her plan to speak to Adrian. Gene has rattled her. She's getting a strong urge to retreat and leave the shelter altogether.

Her pace slows as she weighs the options of heading into the dining room or retreating to her bedroom. Adrian appears in the hall.

She flexes her fingers and wears her best customer service smile. When his eyebrows lift, she drops the smile and shrugs. *He always sees through me.*

Jazz lifts a hand in a mediocre wave, and says, "Hi."

Adrian moves towards her. "What are you after? Did you keep your identity secret because you want to take over the site for one of your gyms? Just because we're short on cash doesn't mean—"

"Adrian." She lifts her hands to stop his line of thinking. "I'm not after the shelter."

He points a finger between her eyes. "I don't trust people like you. What's the angle?"

Her hands collapse over her heart. "I'm not trying to steal this place from you."

Adrian shakes his head and pushes past her towards his office.

"Adrian," she calls out. Her body slumps, angry at herself for not being honest with him. For not telling him how she could save this place.

Family

Adrian throws the papers off his desk. Frustrated breaths race out of him. After Jazz ran out of the dining room, Gene filled him in on who she really is. Adrian feels every ounce of blood pumping through his veins. His hands make fists and his teeth grit to stop himself from punching the wall.

How could I be so stupid? The betrayal clings to his body and droops his posture. Resentment takes control of his mind as he thinks about the privacy awarded to people who walk through the shelter's door. Who else is under this roof with false pretences? He knew there was something off about Jazz, but he let his attraction for her stop him from digging. She was secretive in a different way from most people. He should have known better and kept his guard up.

He was about to give her access to the shelter's money. The thought makes him sick to his stomach. She's a corporate business person. The type of person he distrusts the most. *Corruption.*

He thinks about the new boy he let in. He sits on his desk, picks up the phone, and dials the number for social services. He promised himself he wouldn't let in another mouth to feed. But seeing the boy made his heartstrings pull. The shine to his eyes told Adrian he needed help. Not to mention the bruises to his face. How could he turn his back? He listens to the on-hold music and knows getting a caseworker to help the boy will give himself one less problem.

There is a knock on his door and he grunts, "Go away."

"Adrian, it's Eddy. Can I come in?"

Adrian scratches his head with the phone receiver and then rests it on his shoulder. "Fine."

Eddy steps into the room, shutting the door behind him. "I just ran into Jazz."

Adrian rolls his eyes, not wanting to talk about her, and slides the phone up to his ear.

"What's going through your mind?" Eddy asks, sitting on a chair and taking his time to meet Adrian's eyes.

"I just need to call someone to take care of this kid."

"What kid?"

"A new one I just let in."

"I thought you—"

"—Just don't," Adrian snaps.

Eddy stands and steps forward. "Hey, it's cool. I know how strong your need to help people is."

"But that won't help the others." His knuckles whiten around the phone. "We won't be able to feed anyone or keep the power on."

"Adrian," Eddy says, holding out an arm toward his friend. "Why don't you put the phone down? You're not in the right frame of mind to make this call."

Adrian tugs away from Eddy. "No."

"Let's just talk about this first."

"I just want to tell them to come."

"Why? It's not like you. You avoid social workers."

Adrian drops the phone and sweeps his hands over his face. "I can't help him."

Eddy pulls his friend into a hug. "Talk to me. You're putting too much stress and responsibility on yourself. Tell me what you need and I'll make the calls."

Adrian rests his chin on Eddy's shoulder, and lets out a breath that had clogged his chest. He shakes his head and pushes away from Eddy. He picks up the phone and says, "No, I gotta do this now."

Eddy moves away, hands slung in his pockets. "You're not alone. Remember that. And Jazz wasn't trying to deceive you."

Adrian snorts a laugh. "You want to help me? Tell her to leave."

Eddy's shoulders droop. "Adrian."

"I don't trust her." Someone answers on the other end of the phone. "Yes hi, it's Adrian Cassidy from the shelter off Jordan Street. I've got a kid here who needs some help."

"Hang up," Eddy whispers.

Adrian bats his hand, giving more details to the agent.

Eddy leans over the table and hits end call.

"What are you doing?"

"Talk to the kid first. We don't even know where he's come from. I get that you don't want to get attached, but let me do it. Maybe he's not that hard on his luck and we can get him back home."

Adrian places the phone in the cradle. "Ok, fine. Get him home."

"Social services is always our last resort," Eddy says, opening the door. "I'm surprised at you. You know what that system is like."

Adrian's posture slumps as he follows Eddy to the door. "I wanted a quick solution. I wasn't thinking."

"You want to help the kid, then don't make the call so hastily." Eddy pats his shoulder. "Introduce me to him?"

"Yeah." Adrian halts in the hallway. "He left to find Jazz."

"You can't judge her just because she has money."

"What is she doing here if she has money?"

Eddy meets his eyes. "Money isn't a barrier to needing help. We are here to help anyone who has run from any kind of abuse. You need to check your prejudice at the door."

"You think I'm prejudiced?"

Eddy lifts his eyebrows and continues down the hall.

"Eddy."

"Everyone has baggage. You still need to unpack yours."

Adrian picks up his pace to follow his friend. "I'm not doing it now. Let's just find the kid."

They move towards the bedrooms as a commotion sounds from the common room.

"What was that?" Eddy asks as Adrian turns and moves toward the common room.

Adrian jogs into the common room and yells, "Hey," as soon as he sees Ferg and Max cornering Gene.

"What?" all three boys reply.

Adrian throws his hands up. "What's going on in here?"

Gene shows his phone screen, attached to a cord plugged into the wall behind him. "I was just showing them a video."

"Check out this kid's phone," Max cheers, gesturing to Gene.

"He's got the latest," Ferg adds, grinning.

Adrian walks up to them, nodding at Gene. "What was the yelling then?"

Max taps Gene's phone and the video replays. "Watch."

Adrian angles his head as he approaches Gene. On the video, a boy rides a scooter in a skate rink. He zooms high into the air and comes down into a horrific landing.

"*Ehck*," Adrian retches, looking away. "Why are you watching that?"

Gene shrugs. "It's the only way I know how to make friends with straight boys."

Ferg pats Gene's back. "And that he did."

Adrian pans across the boys' faces. "So, we're good here?"

"Yep," the boys reply, all smiling and nodding.

Adrian locks eyes with Gene. "Can we talk for a minute?"

Gene's eyes brighten, and he nods eagerly.

Adrian gestures to the couch and Gene follows him over.

"You good?" Eddy asks, walking by the couch.

Adrian nods, knowing Eddy wants him to talk to Gene on his own.

Eddy nods back and moves to the pool table. "Ferg and Maxy, game of pool?"

The boys move over to the pool table with Eddy as Adrian and Gene take the couch.

Adrian's stomach swirls as he readies himself for the first question. "So, how long have you been on the streets?"

Gene shakes his head. "Just yesterday."

"Oh." Adrian's spirits lift with hope. "Were you with family before?"

"Yeah. I left my mum and dad." Gene sighs with frustration. "I just couldn't stay with them."

Adrian winces at the bruise on the side of his face. "It got physical?"

"Yeah. My dad's reaction to me coming out."

Adrian presses his stomach and looks to his knees. "I'm sorry."

Gene sinks into the couch. "I'm just not going to hide who I am anymore."

"That's what your parents want? You to hide your sexuality?"

"More like deny it. They want me to lie about who I am to make themselves feel better."

"How old are you?"

"Fifteen."

"Do you see a way you can work this out with them?"

Gene twists his lips. "Only if I play it straight."

"Has your father gotten physical before yesterday?"

"Not this bad."

Adrian's stomach contracts and throbs. "It'd be great if you could work out a way to go home. Otherwise, we need to call social services, and you don't want to be in the foster care system."

"Maybe it'd be better?"

"No," Adrian says with a slow shake of the head. "I spent years in foster homes. Maiden City can be an unkind place."

"What happened to your family?"

Adrian swallows hard as his mind grows woozy. "They died."

Gene grows a whiter shade of pale. "I'm sorry."

"It was a long time ago," Adrian murmurs, waving a hand to change the subject. "I just want to tell you from experience to try your best not to go into foster care. It would have been good growing up in a proper family."

Gene frowns but nods. "I'll think about it."

Adrian stands and moves toward the doorway. Eddy leaves the pool table and catches up to him, asking, "Everything ok?"

"He'll think about going back home to his parents."

Eddy points to his cheek. "So the bruise came from the streets?"

Adrian's temples ache. He turns to the door and moves into the hall.

"What about Jazz?"

Adrian turns back to Eddy, waiting for him to elaborate.

"Do you still want her gone?"

Adrian huffs and turns away. "Whatever. She can stay... if she really wants to."

Son

Ethan straightens his tie and smooths his blazer, twirling a bouquet of tulips as he strides the fourth floor corridor of Maiden City University Hospital.

He stops by a nurse and taps the bouquet against his chest. "Excuse me, Miss. I'm here to see Darius Abadi. How is he today?"

The nurse smiles, clasping her hands and rocking onto the balls of her feet. "He's doing better, considering. His spirits need lifting, so a visit will do him well."

Ethan lifts his chin, his smile sliding to the right as his gaze pivots to Darius' room. "Excellent." He turns back to the nurse and nods. "Thank you, Miss. You are a treasure."

"Oh," the young nurse blushes, touching her ash blonde ponytail. "It was nothing."

Ethan gives her a wink, which makes her gasp enthusiastically, and then spins towards Darius' room. His heart swells when his charms work to get people to act the way he wants. Jazz didn't cooperate, and it was a misstep he didn't expect. The good feeling quickly turns into a seething rage as Jazz's face clouds his vision.

He knocks on the door twice as it creaks open. "How's the patient?" he asks, stepping into the room. He walks to the foot of the bed, taking in the beeping sounds and LED signals on the machines. "You're looking well."

"What have I told you about lying?" Darius answers in a raspy voice. He folds his arms across his chest, coughing weakly as tubes run into his nose and leads suction to his chest.

"I don't know if we've ever discussed lying," Ethan says, moving to a chair and making himself comfortable. He places the bouquet on a table, saying, "I'll have a nurse get a vase with water."

Darius winces, batting a hand.

"So," Ethan says, lifting his palms up and out. "Are we having a mentor session, or not? What is your wisdom on lying?"

Darius groans, staring intensely at the ceiling.

Ethan smirks, unbuttoning his blazer. "Ok, it's your choice. Guess you didn't impart that knowledge on Jazz either."

Darius scowls, and the machine at his bedside intensifies with beeps.

Ethan stands and moves towards the window. "Thought I might run into her here."

"No," Darius says, his voice strained and hoarse. "My daughter has not checked in on her ailing father."

Ethan moves to the bed and scoops Darius' hand in his. "You know I'll always stand by you."

Darius' face softens and his weepy eyes meet Ethan's. "Thank you... Son."

Ethan's jaw flexes. He sniffs, purses his lips and nods. "You know," he whispers, "the doctors gave me the impression you need to relieve yourself from massive stress. I can take the reins at HQ. You taught me well. Let me act as CEO in your absence."

Darius gazes at the ceiling, thoughts twitching his eyes.

"You know I can do it. And, actually... it might be better for your health if you stay away from Ultimate ME all together." Ethan squeezes Darius' hand. "Let me take over, officially."

"We have to wait for the board meeting."

Ethan leans over Darius and waits for him to lock eyes. "Bring it forward."

Ethan watches the apprehension and confusion dull Darius' eyes. He looms over his mentor until his eyes settle and he squeezes his hand back.

"You'll name me successor?" Ethan whispers.

Darius removes his hand from Ethan's and tilts to face the window. "This near death experience leads me wanting to be closer to my daughter. I can't Ethan... I will only feel comfort from an Abadi leading Ultimate ME."

Ethan rises from Darius' side, and smooths his blazer as he walks the length of the bed. His jaw strains as he attempts to keep his fury inside. "I will never be good enough for you."

"Don't be like that."

Ethan spins on his wing-tips and meets Darius' eyes. "I'm the one keeping the company afloat, but you'd prefer to name a woman who's abandoned us."

Darius frowns and lowers his gaze.

You want Jazz, I'll get Jazz. I'll find her and keep her silent, behind me.

He texts Ignacio. ***Do your job. I need her NOW.***

Donation

"**Jazz**, man, we running outta stuff to cook in this kitchen," Hector says at the open fridge. "This ain't good."

Jazz moves over to him and her mouth runs dry. "I can find some money," Jazz whispers.

"How you gonna do that?"

"Don't worry. I can take care of it."

Hector crosses his arms. "I heard something about you."

Jazz purses her lips and pats Hector's arm. "I can fix it."

"Jazz," Eddy says, pushing open the kitchen door. "Can I speak with you?"

"Sure," she says, moving away from Hector. "How's Adrian?"

"He'll come around."

"He's angry?" Jazz flexes her fingers. "I didn't mean to hurt him. I just didn't want to be me for a while."

"I get it. He just has a tough time with the top end of town."

"He can't lump us all in together."

"Like you shouldn't judge everyone here the same way?"

She sighs and nods. "Ok, you got me there. You don't know until you're in it." She fixes her ponytail and asks, "Any word on Myra and Taz? Do you think they could have just gone out for the morning? Maybe to see family?"

"I haven't seen them or heard anything," Eddy says. "I'm sorry."

"The Arab girl?" Hector asks, washing his hands.

Jazz turns to him. "Yeah. You know something?"

"I saw her run out of here while I was prepping breakfast," Hector says.

"Run out?" Jazz repeats.

"I thought it was a little weird," Hector says with a shrug. "But we get that a lot. I know not to ask questions."

Jazz rushes to Hector. "She's running from an abusive partner. She needs protecting!"

"Jazz," Eddy says, pulling her from Hector.

Hector lifts his arms in defence. "*Oi*! You can't get mad at me for giving people their privacy. I been here a long time, Missy."

"*Missy?*" Jazz snaps, wriggling from Eddy's grip. "Eddy, let me go!"

"Come outside with me and get some air," Eddy says, letting her go.

"Fine," she says, storming out of the kitchen and into the back alley. She groans with frustration, throwing her arms out wide and high.

"Take some deep breaths," Eddy says, following her out. When Jazz kicks some bags of rubbish by the dumpster, he sighs and says, "That won't do any good."

"Nothing I do is any good!" she yells. "So why even bother?"

"Is this about Myra or Adrian?" Eddy asks, perching on an upturned milk crate.

Jazz grumbles, ripping her hair from the ponytail. "I just wanted to help."

"You are helping."

"Everyone sees the spoilt heiress now."

"I see the woman who works damn hard to continue her father's legacy. The woman who came here blind and now gets her hands dirty without complaint. Be proud you got a doctor to see Myra before she left."

"I should just leave and mail a cheque."

"You think your money is more valuable than your time?"

"Adrian needs money. The men in my life just want to use me, so why should he be any different?" She leans against a dumpster, not worried about the sticky brown cluster beside her. "My father wants me in senior management because of my surname. Ethan wants to marry me, to use my last name to become CEO."

"You and Adrian need to talk," Eddy says, standing. "I can't speak for him, but I've never known him to use anyone."

Jazz smirks at herself, pulling her hair behind her ears. "Maybe I bring it out in men."

"Jazz, I'm sorry they have treated you this way in the past, but please try to stay open-minded." He holds his hand out. "Will you come back inside with me?"

Jazz eyes his hand and slides her hands into the pockets of her second-hand jeans. "I'll go in."

Eddy drops his hand and smiles. "Good."

They walk back into the kitchen and move into the dining room.

Jazz halts. "Oh," she says as she locks eyes on Adrian who is at the entrance from the hall. "Hi."

Adrian finds her eyes but diverts them to Eddy. "Case workers are here."

"What?" Eddy says in a panic.

"What's going on?" Jazz asks Eddy.

Eddy walks past her and hurries towards Adrian. "Why are they here?"

Adrian shrugs and Jazz notices the glassiness to his eyes. "That phone call."

Eddy groans. "He's got no chance now."

Eddy rushes down the hall and Adrian moves to follow, until Jazz calls out, "Please wait."

Adrian stops mid-step. His back flexes as he considers turning back to face Jazz.

"Please," she whispers.

He turns and leans against the doorframe. "What?"

She winces as the hurt pangs in her heart. "You found out who I really am." Her voice warbles as she steps towards him, her eyes stinging with the threat of tears. "I come from a wealthy family. I can help financially."

Adrian's expression gives nothing away.

She grits her teeth and rubs her lips together. "I can give a donation."

"Thanks," he says, pulling himself off the doorframe. "That'd be helpful." He turns and leaves down the hall.

She closes her eyes tight, but a tear escapes, tumbling down her cheek. "I'm sorry."

Pure contempt would have been better than no reaction at all. He was cold. She never meant to come across as deceptive. She never imagined she could hurt someone so much. Someone she is genuinely growing strong feelings for.

Comfortable

"**Gene**, you are a minor," the female caseworker says. In his overwhelmed state, Gene didn't take in her or the man's names. "You need to go back into your parents' care or you will become a ward of the state."

"A ward of the state?" Gene asks, his lip upturning. "What does that mean?"

"The city would be your legal guardian," the man says, flipping through paperwork on his lap. "You'd be assigned to a group home."

"Your parents filed a report with the police department about your disappearance," the woman says. "They want you back home, as do we."

"Gene," the tall blonde guy he'd seen with Adrian says, running into the common room. He skids to a stop beside Gene. "Are you ok?"

"And you are?" the male caseworker asks.

"Eddy Barnes," Eddy says, sitting by Gene. "I'm the counsellor here, and we're capable of getting Gene home. We don't need your help."

"Well, that's not really up to you, Mr Barnes," the woman says, flashing Eddy her ID. "My associate Mr Duban and I work for the government and outrank you."

Eddy smirks. "*This* the government will act on, but not helping us keep the shelter running."

"Whatever you are looking for monetary wise from the government," Mr Duban says, "it's not our department. Now, Gene, is it safe for you at home?"

Gene sucks in a breath, eyes darting between the caseworkers and Eddy. He is feeling more and more like a burden on all involved. "I guess?"

"Don't pressure him," Eddy says. He gestures to Gene. "Look at his face."

The woman, Miss Eden it said on her ID, leans in. "Did a parent do this to you?"

Gene touches his face, wincing at the biting tenderness. "Not all of it. Some were from guys at school."

"Did you antagonise these people?" Mr Duban asks.

Gene chokes, feeling punched in the gut. "By being gay?"

"It relates to your sexuality?" Miss Eden asks.

"The guys at school thought I made a mockery of them." Gene touches under his eye. "And my dad wanted me to say I was lying about being gay."

"So, your parents will feel more comfortable if you conceal your homosexuality while living under their roof?" Miss Eden adds.

Gene swallows uncomfortably. "I guess."

"Do you think you can do that?" Mr Duban asks. "So we can keep you at home until you are of legal age?"

"Hang on," Eddy interjects.

"No, I can," Gene interrupts Eddy.

"You shouldn't have to lie about who you are," Eddy says.

"Adrian made a good point that I should try to make it work."

Eddy's eyes widen. "Adrian said that?"

Gene shrugs. "He was trying to help."

The caseworkers stand, and Miss Eden says, "We need to add to our report and we'll be back. Sit tight, Gene."

Eddy stands, folding his arms. "You and I need to talk this out before you go anywhere with them. Wait for me, yeah? I need to find Adrian."

Gene nods. "Ok, I'll wait."

Date

Adrian slings his hands in the pockets of his trousers as he walks toward the common room.

"You!" Eddy yells, pointing to Adrian as he marches up the hall. "My office, now."

"Ed, I don't—"

Eddy grabs Adrian's arm and spins him around. "Not negotiable." He pushes him through the doorway of his office and shuts the door behind them. "Did you tell Gene to play it straight with his parents?"

Adrian huffs and leans against the wall. "I was just saying he should do what he can to stay out of foster care."

"What's gotten into you?" Eddy asks, arms crossing against his chest. "This is usually what you would fight against, not set up."

Adrian's face falls into his hands as he slides down the wall.

Eddy moves to Adrian and crouches in front of him. "You need a better way to manage your stress. You can't continue this way."

"It's hard," he whispers through cupped hands.

"I know, man. I know."

"Jazz has thrown me. I was really starting to trust her. But she's from the most despicable class in Maiden City."

"Is it really fair to judge Jazz by her status? Isn't that what you fear most? Think about if she judges you by your past or by your parents' actions?"

Adrian grits his teeth and nods. He wipes his hands over his face and then stands, shaking out his limbs. "I should give her the benefit of the doubt. Hear her out."

Eddy stands, smiling. "That'd be a good start."

Adrian feels the colour returning to his skin. "She still here?"

"I believe so. Kitchen with Hector?"

Adrian runs his hands through his hair and blows out a heavy breath. He drops his hands, nods, and moves toward the door. "Ok."

"I'll check on Gene," Eddy says, following him out.

"Tell him I'll see him after Jazz." Adrian rubs his guilt-ridden stomach. "I need to apologise."

Eddy pats Adrian's shoulder and turns down the hall.

Adrian straightens his back and moves toward the dining room. He finds Hector wiping down some tables and asks if he's seen Jazz.

"Out back," Hector says, gesturing towards the kitchen.

Adrian moves into the kitchen and his stomach drops when there's no one in sight. He turns to the back door and drags his feet forward. When he reaches for the door, it pushes open.

"Oh." He jumps back as Jazz walks through the doorway. His heart pounds as she brushes the hair off her face. "How are you?"

She folds her arms. "Ok."

"Look, I jumped to conclusions about you," he blurts. "I'm sorry, I shouldn't have done that. It wasn't fair."

Jazz looks to her shoes. "No, it wasn't."

Adrian frowns, hating her low mood. "You have a right to privacy, just like everyone else who stays here. I got a little paranoid, and that's on me."

She looks up. "What is your problem with money?"

"It's not exactly the money. It's what it does to people." He takes a step back to allow her into the kitchen. "Is there any way I can help you with what you're running from?"

Jazz sighs against the doorframe, slipping her hands behind her back. "I'm sorry I didn't open up. I was enjoying being invisible."

"Invisible?"

"I've never been somewhere where no one knows who I am."

"So, who are you?" Adrian says, propping himself against a steel bench. "Gene says you run a big fitness company."

"My father does." Her eyes shift to the right. "He's stepping down and needs to name a successor."

"And it'll be you?"

"There's a board of directors who have the final say. They don't want me."

Adrian folds his arms. "Do you want to run the company?"

Jazz nods, but her expression is less than confident. "I've been working towards it my entire life." Her fingers flex by her sides. "I just thought I'd have more time."

Adrian nods. "You are young to be up for the job. Is that why the board what's someone else?"

"Hopefully." She chews her lip. "Or it's because I'm female."

"That shouldn't matter," Adrian says, shifting his weight, uncomfortable with how likely a factor it could be. "You've worked for your father as soon as you were old enough?"

She nods, preoccupied with her own thoughts.

"And it's your birthright."

"That's my thought." Her eyes are pure worry when they meet his.

"You don't look like you want it."

She stands up straight and flicks her hair off her shoulders. "No, I do."

"Ok. So, you came here because you needed time to figure out your decision with your father's company?"

Jazz turns towards the door. "I didn't exactly choose to come here, remember. I was blackout drunk."

Adrian unravels his arms and whispers, "Wanna talk about it?"

Jazz moves further into the kitchen and stops a few steps away from Adrian. "I was running from the man taking away the company."

Adrian's chest tightens as his heart pounds harder. "He was with you?"

"He proposed to me."

Adrian's heart drops. "Oh."

"To use me."

"What?"

"My father wants me in senior management because of my surname. Ethan sees me as his highest competition to get my father's approval. He wants to shut me up."

Knots run up Adrian's back as he takes a step toward Jazz. "Did he get you drunk?"

"Only by speaking with his stupid voice." When the dread doesn't leave Adrian's face, Jazz grows solemn. "No, I asked for the drinks. It was all me. He asked me to slow down."

"But he was threatening you?"

"He wants to control me." Jazz shakes her head, rolling her eyes. "But he can't."

Adrian nods, seriousness weighting his expression. "No, he can't."

Jazz steps in close and runs a hand down his arm. "I'm ok. Thank you for bringing me inside when I was beyond myself."

"I'm sorry I jumped to conclusions about you. You've been working so hard here and you're fitting in. I should have known better."

Jazz steps back and smiles. "You were in shock. It was totally acceptable. I came in here loaded with judgements. We're human."

"It's my whole job," Adrian says, trying to lighten the tension. "I should have been better."

"Well, now you know who I am and why I know about business," Jazz says, fixing her hair behind her ear. "I would really like to help you save this place. If you'll let me."

Adrian's mouth runs dry as he watches her fingers play at the soft waves of her hair. He gulps and nods. "Yes, I'd like that. Maybe we could talk over dinner?"

"You want to talk money in front of everyone?"

He shakes his head, smiling. "They don't need me around every night. We can have dinner just us. Meet me in my office?"

Her eyebrows lift and her eyes brighten. "Lovely. It's a date." She lowers her gaze and laughs. "I mean, it's a deal."

Adrian laughs, seeing the colour change in her cheeks. "See you then. I need to go check on a kid."

Heart

Adrian rushes into the common room and Eddy puts his hand up, and says, "It's ok, we got them to back off."

"The social workers?" Adrian asks, puffing.

"We told them Gene needed time to work out what he wanted to say to his parents." Eddy looks at Adrian sideways. "You ok? You look flushed."

Adrian waves off the question and scoots next to Gene on the couch. "You ok?"

Eddy tells them he has an appointment with Tessa and leaves for the hall.

"I'm ok, but seriously, are you ok?" Gene asks, scrutinising Adrian's features.

Adrian runs a hand through his hair. "I was worried about you."

"Ok?" Gene says sceptically. "What were you doing beforehand?"

Adrian laughs. "What are you fishing for?"

Gene narrows his eyes, waiting for Adrian to tell him what he wants to hear.

Adrian turns his head. "Would you stop looking at me like that? I was talking to Jazz, ok."

"Knew it!" Gene cheers. "You like her, huh?"

Adrian wipes his brow. "She's pretty, but—"

"—Pretty?" Gene repeats. "Jazz Abadi is not pretty, she's a goddess."

Adrian turns back to Gene. "You know a lot about her?"

Gene pulls out his phone and scrolls through Collage. "Only every outfit she's ever worn to every event ever."

"Wow," Adrian murmurs, watching Gene's moving screen. "She goes to a lot of parties."

"How do you not know about her?"

Adrian taps the screen. "Well, I don't have one of these things."

"What? A Collage account?" Gene asks, but then his dark brown eyes widen. "Do you mean a *phone*? You don't own a phone? How is that possible?"

Adrian smirks and shrugs. "I just don't."

"Good lord. You really are shut off from the world, aren't you?"

"I dunno. I meet a lot of people."

"I guess. But no one like Jazz, am I right?"

"She sends me dizzy."

"So, why don't you go back and talk to her more?"

"Because I'm here to check on you."

"I'm fine. You need to get to know her."

"We're having dinner tonight."

Gene leaps from the couch. "This is huge. What are you gonna wear?"

"What?"

Gene's face screws up and he gestures to Adrian's jeans and t-shirt. "You're not going to dinner in that."

Adrian stands and says, "It's just dinner in my office. No big deal."

"No big deal?" Gene repeats, going up an octave. "You're having a private dinner with Jazz Abadi, one of the most influential heiresses in Maiden City.”

“Why are you trying to freak me out?”

“I’m trying to make you see the light.” Gene loops his arm around Adrian’s. “I heard there’s a room of clothes somewhere here. Show me. I’ll fix you.”

“Fix me?”

“Uh, enhance you, is what I mean.”

“I really don’t know,” Adrian says, letting Gene drag him out of the room.

“Trust me. You wanna make a good impression, don’t you?”

“She’s met me.”

“But does she know you?”

“*Ugh*, fine.”

Adrian shows Gene to the donated clothes, and his disgust is vivid on his face.

“This is how you treat your clothes?” Gene winces.

“They’re just clothes.”

“*Just?*” Gene bats a hand and wades through the clothes. “It hurts me. It physically hurts me.”

“Anyone ever told you, you’re overly dramatic?”

Gene puffs his chest, shooting a look back at Adrian. “*Duh.*”

Adrian’s body loosens, and he slouches with a laugh. “Ok, Genie, what do you recommend?”

“You don’t have any nice clothes you wear for special occasions?”

“I wouldn’t say I have any special occasions... but, I guess, I have a suit I wear for meetings.”

“Oh?” Gene grows enthusiastic. “Tailored for you?”

“*What* for me?”

“Boy, lemme guess, it’s two-sizes too big for you?”

“Well, it’s–”

"–*Ugh.*" Gene lifts a hand, closing his eyes. "I'm now assuming you own no clothes."

Adrian laughs, folding his arms and leaning against the wall. "Ok, go for it."

Gene tilts his head, running his eyes up and down Adrian.

Adrian rocks his jaw. "What are you doing?"

"You're a good-looking guy. You should act like it."

Adrian pulls himself off the wall. "I don't know what that means."

"If you show off your assets, people will take you seriously."

"Believe me, that's not something I'm interested in. The people I see every day do not give a damn what I look like. And I don't care what they look like."

"And what about your meetings? Who are they with? What are they for?"

Adrian moans, feeling hit by a freight train.

"Are you all right?"

Adrian shrugs. "I had to go into a government office to ask for grant money. It's nothing you need to worry about."

Gene grows serious. "No, tell me."

"We have to shut this place down," Adrian says, sadness weighing down his shoulders. "We don't have any money to keep it open."

"I saw you turning people away," Gene says in a small voice.

"Sorry, I shouldn't put this on you."

"*Please*, I'm too nosey to keep out."

Adrian laughs. "Yeah, I'm realising that. Anyway, Jazz thinks she knows some ways to keep the place going."

Gene beams. "That's great. So tonight is a big deal in a few ways. Ok, let me work my magic on you."

Adrian shakes his head, smiling. "What am I getting myself into?"

"I'm just getting you ready for a special night. You like Jazz, right?"

"Sure, she's great."

"Just make sure you speak from the heart. Don't make it all about business."

"I need help with this place, though."

"I know. That's important, but open up too. You two look good together."

Adrian's stomach flips, and he laughs. "Ok, relax. You're making me nervous."

Gene laughs. "Ok, sorry. Hey, this might actually work. I need an iron."

Wished

Gene hurries when he spots Jazz in the hallway. "Jazz! Ah, Miss Abadi. Wait up."

Jazz turns and smirks. "Just Jazz is fine."

Gene wipes his brow and grins. "It's still so surreal I've met you. Do you have a minute to talk?"

"Sure. What's up?" Jazz gestures ahead. "I was just going to my bedroom. Do you mind if we go in there?"

Gene's insides buzz. "Yes, please."

"You're an excitable young man, aren't you?"

"Um, do you know how many times I've looked at your Collage feed and wished to transport into your bedroom?"

"Well, don't get too excited," Jazz says, leading him into the room. "It's a dorm room for me and Tessa with nothing I own."

Gene deflates as he takes in the desolate room. "Yeah, not exactly what I pictured."

Jazz *humphs* and picks up something from the edge of her bed. "Well, except this. This is mine."

The buzzing inside him returns and Gene edges to Jazz's bed with interest. "What is that?"

"I was wearing this dress when I ended up here," Jazz says, letting the material spill from her hands and hang against her. "I don't know why I haven't chucked it out. It's torn and filthy."

"No way," Gene says, grabbing the material. "You can't throw this out. This is vintage sheath. Hang on." He tilts his head, taking a closer inspection. "This is the dress they photographed you in, going into Overity. Is it true you were there with Ethan Roth?"

Jazz drops the dress, which Genes catches and cradles like a newborn, and huffs. "Don't remind me."

"He's who you're running from?"

Jazz sits on the bottom bunk and lifts an eyebrow as she looks at Gene. "You're very perceptive."

Gene shrugs with a smirk. "It's a gift." He looks at her sideways. "The photos of you leaving Overity weren't as flattering."

Jazz groans and collapses her face into her hands. "Oh no, the paparazzi snapped me leaving?"

"Don't worry. You're still a babe. So, what are you wearing tonight?"

Jazz lifts her head. "Tonight?"

"Your dinner with Adrian."

"You know about that?"

"I just had to get it through Adrian's head that it's a big deal. Don't tell me I need to sort you out, too."

Jazz stands, her almond eyes enlarging. "He thinks tonight is a big deal?"

Gene smiles and wriggles his eyebrows. "Don't you?"

Gene notices a warmth highlighting her high cheekbones.

He rubs the fabric between his fingers and says, "I can fix this."

"Really?"

"I've seen the donated clothes and think you're wearing the best thing here."

Jazz laughs. "Me too. But how will you fix this?"

"I can wash it in a sink, I've seen a hair dryer that I hope to God works, and," he pauses and gulps as he looks at her, "do you mind if I cut it?"

"Cut it?"

"Alter it. Make it shorter to get rid of this tear."

Jazz nods. "I was going to toss it. If you can fix it, go ahead."

"Perfection. Lord, I'm altering a dress for Jazz Abadi. Am I still standing?" he rushes, holding his forehead.

"Stop being silly," Jazz says with a laugh as she moves to the mirror and combs her fingers through her hair.

"So you'll save this place?"

"I'll try."

"What makes you want to do that?"

Jazz looks over her shoulder at him, her face serious. "They're so accepting. This is the first place people treated me well despite my name and money."

"It's crazy they didn't know who you are. Did you know Adrian doesn't own a phone?"

Jazz's eyes narrow. "How is that possible?"

Gene throws his arms up. "Beats me."

Jazz turns back to the mirror. "Explains why he doesn't follow me, I guess."

"He's a good guy, isn't he?"

Jazz smiles at her reflection, and whispers, "One of the best."

"Try to loosen up tonight," Gene says, moving towards the doorway. "Don't make it entirely about business and finances. Have a good time."

Jazz nods at him. "I will. Good luck with the dress."

"Thanks. I'm gonna raid the place for scissors and something resembling thread."

Lucky

Jazz fixes her hair in soft waves over her shoulder, and they cascade over her chest. She was apprehensive about wearing this dress again after the state she'd left it in, but Gene did an amazing job, almost convincing her it is a new dress.

She takes in a long breath and notices her hands tremble. She frowns and wonders why she's acting so nervously. She's always conducted herself in such a strong and confident manner for business meetings. She then takes in her attire. She laughs and shakes her head. *This is new*. She's never gone into a meeting wondering if it was a date. She never let romance play into life before. Hell, she was proposed to at her last meeting and didn't lose her cool.

Her teeth grit. *Well, I got drunk and blacked-out.* Her stomach tosses with disgust at the memory of Ethan's actions.

She flexes her fingers and pushes the memory aside. She smiles as Adrian's face fills the space in my mind.

"Ok, here goes nothing," she says to her reflection.

She controls her breaths, the same way she would during a run, on the way to Adrian's office. *The only room I haven't been in yet.*

The door is ajar, and she lightly taps at it. Adrian's frame hunches over a table and when he moves away, Jazz realises he is lighting a candle.

"Hey, come on in," he says as Jazz pushes the door open.

"Hi."

"Wow, you look so fancy," Adrian says, his eyes running up and down her dress.

She smooths down her newly altered dress and bites her lip. "I do?"

Adrian moves his eyes up to hers and smiles. "Beautiful, I mean. You look pretty."

Jazz smiles and takes in his dress shirt and pleated trousers. "I could say the same about you. Very handsome."

"Thanks," he says bashfully, gesturing to a chair. "Well, you're here to save this place, I needed to dress up for you."

"You didn't need to do anything," Jazz says, taking a seat. She giggles under her breath as he pushes her chair in for her.

"This is probably pretty shabby compared to what you're used to," Adrian says, rounding the table to relight the candle. "There's not much light in here and Maria found this candle for me. It's probably dumb."

"It's not dumb. It's lovely. Almost perfect in a topsy-turvy way."

Adrian sets the lighter down once the wick stays lit and laughs as he sits across the table. "You don't need to lie. This isn't perfect."

Jazz shrugs, her smile sliding to the left. "It's a nice change of pace."

"Do you go to those fancy balls held by the Mayor?"

"I've been to a few. My family is close with the Walsh family."

"*Whoah.*" Adrian leans in with interest. "What are they like?"

"The balls? They can be stuffy. You need to dress and act a certain way. There's a lot of talk of money and business. In a lot of ways, it's very fake."

Adrian's expression drops. "Oh. I was hoping you'd say they were fun."

Jazz laughs. "Well, I guess some girls find it fun. I'm just not one for getting excited to dress up."

"You always look so nice though."

"I do it, but it's not for fun. It's for an image."

"Oh."

"You must judge me harshly for playing a role. Like I'm a fake."

Adrian shakes his head. "No, I don't."

"Adrian, you flipped out when you found out I'm an heiress."

"Ok, I might have a few thoughts about rich people that made me do that."

Jazz sits back in her chair and looks around the room for the first time. The walls are chipped and cracked, exposing the outside brick. The air is stale. Cobwebs cover the overhead light, which is littered with dead bugs. But what steals Jazz's attention is a skinny fold-out bed with a flimsy mattress pushed against the wall.

"You sleep in here?" she asks abruptly.

"Yeah, this is my room."

Jazz turns back to him. "I assumed you had an office *and* a bedroom."

"No, I have them both in one. I don't want to take up that much room."

"You deserve more space than this."

"Nah, it's enough. We need space to help people. That's if we can keep the place running."

"You can. I have a few ideas."

Adrian plays with the cuffs of his shirt and keeps his eyes down.

"You seem nervous."

"You're rich."

"I'm the same person you've spoken to all week."

He laughs. "Yeah, the person I knew there was something off about."

She twitches. "Off?"

He smiles. "Different."

"That we are."

"I try to treat everyone the same. I didn't want to freak out because you're from money, but I've had bad experiences with people from your side of the city." He fidgets in his seat. "I wanted to keep my cool, but then Gene told me it was a huge deal to have one-on-one time with you, and he freaked me out. He kept saying your full name like you were royalty or something. Sorry, I still don't know how to pronounce your last name. What is it?"

"Abadi."

"Abadi. Ok, I'll remember that. Jazz Abadi."

Jazz giggles. "Ok, good. What's your last name?"

"Cassidy."

"Well, nice to officially meet you, Adrian Cassidy."

"Like we're meeting the real us?"

"I'm ready to put all my cards out on the table if you are."

"I guess I'm gonna have to. I need your help."

"How did you start running this place?" Jazz asks, looking around at the room. "Did you start it up, or take it over from someone? It's hard to get real estate in the city." When Adrian flinches, Jazz is quick to add. "I promise I'm not trying to acquire the site."

Adrian smiles and lets out a weighted breath. "You were honest with me. I should do the same thing."

"You've been lying about something?"

"*Geez*, you know how to throw out the questions to make people feel like they are on trial."

Jazz's shoulders droop. "*Oops.*"

Adrian grins. "I'm teasing you. No, I haven't been lying, just haven't been open." He stretches his neck side-to-side, preparing to lay it all out. "I came here after leaving a group home."

"What's a group home?"

Adrian splutters a laugh. "Wow, we really are from different worlds. It's foster care, but when you're not in a family, just living in a place run by the city."

Jazz's demeanour strains. "You didn't have your own family?"

"Just their baggage." He shifts in his chair. "My parents died."

Jazz's cheeks pinch as her eyes gleam with tears. "That's awful, I'm sorry."

"Thanks. It was a long time ago."

Jazz's stomach pangs as she takes in the sorrow paling his face. "I lost my mother a long time ago too."

"I'm sorry. It never matters how long ago it was, it still hurts, doesn't it?"

Jazz sniffs back a tear and smiles. In a small voice, she asks, "Can I ask what happened to your parents?"

"They were shot," he says flatly.

Jazz's heart plummets. "What? Really?"

He nods, grinding his teeth as he looks to the floor. "I saw it happen."

Jazz rushes off her chair and races to his side. She kneels beside him, touching his forearm. "Oh, Adrian, I'm so sorry. No one should ever have to see that."

He meets her eyes and takes her hand. He clears his throat and says, "Is it bad to say I'm better off without them?"

"What?"

"They weren't good people, Jazz."

Jazz rubs her heart, staring into his eyes to his soul, waiting for him to elaborate.

Adrian rubs his forehead. "They were criminals. They made me tag along to help them steal things in tight places."

Jazz's chin drops. "They forced you to steal?"

"I was a kid. I didn't know it was wrong." He pauses, closing his eyes and shaking his head. "Until the heat started increasing."

"Was it the police that shot them?"

He nods. "They were tracking them down after we did too many burglaries in a row."

Jazz's eyes sting with tears. "You weren't hurt, were you?"

"No, they just took me away." He looks at her with apprehension. "What happened to your mother?"

Her sharp breath lodges in her throat. Her voice quivers as she replies, "She died giving birth to me."

Sadness blankets Adrian's face as his shoulders collapse.

"I'm the reason she's dead."

"Jazz, no," Adrian whispers, brushing her jaw. "It's not your fault."

A tear rolls down her face. The mix of their individual pain proving too much for her to bear. "My father would be better off if I was the one who didn't make it."

Adrian leans in and scoops her into his embrace. Jazz stays limp, letting him hold her up. She nestles her head against his chest. The warmth of his body and his strong heartbeat steadying her calm.

His hand brushes back her thick, black hair, and he whispers, "No one would be better off without you."

Jazz's heart both swells and tears. Heartbroken, yet so touched. She pulls out of Adrian's arms and brings herself to standing.

She backs to a wall and leans against it. "I just need to stand for a minute, if that's ok."

Adrian turns in his chair to face her. "Sure, that's ok."

"Can we have a change of pace?" Jazz asks, rubbing her confused heart.

"Change of pace?"

"I was thinking, this place is falling apart," Jazz says, running her fingers over the exposed brick. "It will take a lot of money to complete the repairs. Perhaps moving to a new site would be cheaper in the long run."

"*Whoah*, how do you think we could afford that?"

"Not for you to buy or rent. A donation." Jazz's tears dry up as she charges her business brain. "A site donated by a corporation."

Adrian shakes his head, folding his arms. "Nah-uh. We can't be under a corporation's thumb. No way."

"They wouldn't run it. They'd donate the site and then the transaction would be over."

Adrian unravels his arms, interest relaxing his expression. "You think that could happen?"

"I have plenty of connections in the Business District. I'm sure I could pull something off."

"Wow."

Jazz moves towards the table and slides the papers she brought with her toward Adrian. "I made a plan, if you want to look over it."

Adrian slides the papers back. "Oh, it's ok. I'm sure you've got it sorted."

Jazz plants her fingers on the papers so they stay on his side of the table. "No, don't take my word for it. You should read it over. I've got a pen for you to add notes. Everything is ultimately up to you."

Adrian scoots his chair back, avoiding her eyes. "I can't read that."

"What do you mean? You don't want to? You can keep it and get back to me later, if you prefer."

"No. I mean, I can't read it." His jaw flexes and he meets her eyes. "I can't read."

The air smacks out of Jazz. Her hands press on her chest. "How is that possible?"

Adrian clasps his hands, dropping his gaze as he shrugs. "I never went to school."

Jazz steps away from the table, her knees knocking and hands trembling. All her emotions from moments earlier resurface and her eyes fog with tears. An ugly moan gurgles out of her.

"Whoah, Jazz," Adrian says, jumping off his seat with urgency to get to her side. He places a hand on her back and the other squeezes her hand. "Sit down."

Adrian edges her backward, and she sits slowly on the creaky bed.

"It's not fair," she croaks through a laboured breath. "I got everything. I never thought of myself as lucky, but you've had it so much worse than me."

"Hey, don't be like that." Adrian brushes back her hair and her eyes fall closed with the perfect pressure of his touch.

"Education is so powerful," she whispers with a lump in her throat. "I'm getting ready to start my second university degree and have more study plans after that. It gives me so much pain you haven't had that right."

Adrian pulls her close and rubs her bare arm. "Well, I can read a few words. Eddy's taught me a bit. But it's hard to learn. It gives me a headache, so I stopped trying."

"You should try again," she says, placing a hand on his thigh.

"Maybe I will. I dunno, it just didn't seem important."

"It's important. It gives you more choice and freedom. Will you try?"

His breathy laugh tickles the skin below her ear. "I can try."

Jazz clutches his hand, and the warmth makes her smile. She looks up and is mesmerised by the candlelight dancing in his big brown eyes. His thumb draws a small circle on the edge of her hand, and she watches the corners of his lips tug upwards. Her heart leaps to her throat as a powerful urge pulls her body closer to his. She gulps, closes her eyes and pouts her lips.

A loud knock at the door springs her eyes open and the pair break apart.

Safer

"Adrian," a frantic voice says as the door bursts open. Max runs into the room, chest heaving. "It's DJ. You gotta come quick."

Adrian drops Jazz's hand and launches off the bed. He turns to her and says, "Stay here and catch your breath."

She stands. "I'm ok, I'll come with you."

Max hurries out the door. "Adrian, come on! Quick!"

The panic in Max's voice sends Adrian to chase after him without another thought on Jazz. He runs after Max and lands in the dining room where DJ's voice bounces off the walls.

Tension fills the room. The small amount of people in the room are scattered and stand in rigid positions. Adrian's eyes dart around the room and find DJ by the food, yelling and slicing a knife through the air in dangerous angles.

Eddy stands a few metres by him, knees bent and hands out, steady and ready. Hector stands motionless in the kitchen doorway, eyes circular with fear.

Adrian edges towards DJ through the frozen onlookers. His stomach clenches as he notices red splashes on the vinyl floor. *Blood.*

His mouth sours with the threat of his stomach contents surging upward. As he takes in more of the scene, he stops dead. Maria is on the ground, holding her shoulder as fresh blood oozes between her fingers.

"What did you do?" Adrian says to DJ, his blood running cold.

"Stay back!" DJ yells. "Don't come near me!"

"Put the knife down," Adrian says, edging closer to the kid.

DJ points the knife to his abdomen. "Don't come any closer! I'm gonna kill myself."

Gasps of shock fly around the room.

"Adrian," Eddy hisses, pushing his arm back. "Get back."

A hand cuffs around Adrian's wrist, and it makes him jump.

"It's me," Jazz whispers behind him.

Adrian blows out a breath. He clasps her hand as another level of dread escalates the situation. "Get back," he whispers. "I don't want you to get hurt."

"I'm not letting you get hurt," she whispers back, holding him tight, her will shining strong in her eyes.

Adrian looks back at the scared and irrational boy with the knife. He unravels his hand from Jazz's and takes another step forward.

"Get back!" DJ screams.

Adrian lifts his hands in surrender. "I don't want to hurt you, and I don't want you to hurt yourself. *Please*. Please, DJ, put down the knife."

"You!" DJ turns, thrashing the knife in the air. "Stop!"

Adrian looks over his shoulder to see Jazz is the one DJ is threatening. She drops by Maria, ignoring DJ's panicked screams, and puts pressure on Maria's wound.

Adrian heart rate skyrockets. From the corner of his eye he sees Eddy moving toward DJ. As DJ fixates on Jazz, without another moment's thought, Adrian ambushes DJ. He tackles him to the ground and wrestles for the knife. Eddy slides to the ground, struggling to control DJ's wayward arms and gain the knife.

Adrian feels a hot pain sting his arm. He grits through the pain and fights for the knife as Eddy takes hold of DJ, pinning him to the ground. Adrian slams his knee against DJ's wrist and frees the knife.

Adrian sits back on the vinyl floor, puffing as he grips the knife. He looks to his other arm and watches blood drip from his fresh wound.

"Adrian," Jazz cries out.

"I'm ok," he says, wiping away the blood. It was a long cut, but not deep.

"We need to call the police," Eddy says, struggling to keep hold of DJ.

"No," Adrian says in a defeated tone.

"It's not safe," Eddy says, pushing DJ against the floor. "He's not well."

Adrian spins on the floor. "Max!"

Max dashes by his side.

"Can you please call the police?" Adrian asks.

Sadness and terror twists Max's face as he nods.

"You were so brave," Adrian says to him before he leaves the room for a phone. Adrian looks to the table and sees Gene and Ferg huddled beside each other. "You two ok?"

The two shiver as they nod.

Hector rushes to help Eddy, using his size to anchor DJ to the ground and tying his apron around his wrists. "Sorry, he got to the knife before I could stop him."

"It's not your fault," Adrian and Eddy say at once.

With Eddy and Hector having control over DJ, Adrian moves to Jazz and Maria.

"She'll need a doctor," Jazz says, her knuckles almost white from her grip.

"Maria," Adrian says, peeling back Jazz's hands to take her place. "Are you ok?"

Maria groans in pain but nods.

"There's probably a towel or something we could wrap around her arm," Adrian says, and Jazz quickly gets up and races into the kitchen.

When Jazz returns, Adrian takes the clean dish towel from her and ties it around Maria's wounded arm. A red hand print visible on the material.

"The police will send an ambulance," Adrian says to Maria. "You'll be fine."

The police arrive and handcuff DJ. When one officer takes DJ out to their car, the other takes statements from those who witnessed the incident. Adrian is careful not to give any information to imply DJ is dangerous or aggressive, just that he's a scared and misunderstood teenager.

A paramedic checks Adrian's arm, and it only needs a bandage, which they wrap on site. They take Maria to the hospital. The three gashes on her arm and shoulder are deep and in danger of infection.

"She should be out by the morning," the paramedic says, and he and his partner help her out of the building.

Adrian thanks them and then joins Jazz in the kitchen. She is at the sink, scrubbing her hands under scalding water.

Adrian turns on the cold tap and asks her if she's ok.

Jazz shakes her head. "I've never seen anything like that."

Goosebumps line her arms and she shivers. Adrian wraps an arm around her, careful not to touch her with his blood-stained hand.

"Oh," she gasps, turning to him. "Your arm."

Adrian pulls away from her and dips his hands under the water. "I'm ok. It's not that bad."

Jazz wraps the soap with a cloth and begins cleaning Adrian's hand. Adrian smiles at her gentleness and care.

Jazz laughs nervously, placing the soap in his hand. "Sorry, I'm probably not helping."

"Don't be sorry. It was nice."

"That was so scary," she says under her breath. "I can't believe he cut you."

"I've had worse." Adrian lifts his shirt and exposes a long, raised scar on the left side of his abdomen.

"Oh goodness," Jazz gasps, planting a hand on his scar. "Who did that to you?"

He drops his shirt, and she removes her hand. "Someone in my group home who didn't like me."

Tears fill Jazz's eyes. "It's not fair that people have to live like this."

"Don't feel you're better off," Adrian says, taking her hand. "Today you told me someone was trying to force you into marriage."

Jazz's throat warbles with the threat of sobs. "There is something very wrong with this city."

"You guys ok?" Eddy says, entering the kitchen.

"Yeah," Adrian replies. "Are you? How did that all happen?"

Eddy rubs the back of his neck, sighing. "It was fast. I should have seen it coming. He's been declining for the past few days."

"I thought he was doing better," Adrian replies.

"He couldn't stay," Eddy adds quickly, his green eyes full of sadness. "He would have hurt someone or himself."

Adrian nods, his stomach knotting. "Ok."

Eddy tilts his head in Jazz's direction. "You ok?"

She nods. "I will be."

"I'm doing the rounds," Eddy says, walking back into the dining room.

"I should too," Adrian says to Jazz.

Jazz pushes her hair off her face and tries to look brave. "Yeah, it's getting late. Do you want me to help clean up?"

Adrian takes Jazz by the hand and leads her out of the kitchen. "No, you look too shaken up. How about I walk you back to your room? I want to check on Tessa. I'll stay as long as you need me to."

"Thank you," she says and squeezes Adrian's hand. "This certainly wasn't where I thought tonight was headed."

Adrian bites his lip and tries a smile. "Nope, me either."

Hector swirls a mop against the vinyl floor, red streaking the waves of disinfectant and water.

"I'll be back to help," Adrian says as he leads Jazz out of the dining room. "I'm just walking Jazz to her room."

"No worries, brother," Hector says, frowning and shaking his head. "You take your time. I was useless back there. Frozen. I don't mind doing the cleaning up."

"It was a crazy thing," Adrian replies. "Don't be too hard on yourself."

Adrian rubs Jazz's shoulder as they walk down the hall. "You're freezing."

"Must be shock," Jazz murmurs, opening the bedroom door.

They walk inside and Adrian pulls a blanket off a bed and wraps it around Jazz's shoulders.

"You should sit," he says.

Jazz peers at the dress between the folds of the blanket. "I don't care what Gene says, this dress is officially dead now."

"You want to go change or take a shower?" Adrian asks, kneeling by her and staring at the bloodstains on the dress.

"I don't think I could stand in the shower right now," she replies. "I might just sit for a minute and then change."

"Good call."

Jazz stares at her palms, then flips to see the back of her hands. "I don't feel clean."

Adrian brushes her hands. "It's ok. You got all of it."

"Adrian, hey," Tessa says, hurrying into the room. "You two ok?"

Adrian stands. "We're ok. Are you?"

Tessa nods and looks at the ripped part of his shirt, stained red with a bandage underneath. "I can't believe he cut you. Is it serious?"

"No. It hurt at first, but it's fine."

"Ok, good."

"D'you mind if I stay in here for a few minutes?" Adrian asks Tessa. "Jazz is in shock."

"Please," Tessa replies, a shiver knocking her shoulders. "I'd feel safer with you here, too."

Jazz rubs her forehead and lies back on the bed. Adrian sits by her bed and asks if she's in pain.

"Just a headache," Jazz says, eyes closed.

"You want me to go?" he whispers, stroking her hair.

She shakes her head and opens her eyes. "No."

"Shut your eyes," he says. "I'll stay until you fall asleep."

Jazz pulls the blanket tighter around her and sleepily says, "Did you know I was named after my mother?"

His eyes widen as he wonders if she's talking in a dream. "Really?"

She nods, nestling in for sleep. "Yes."

He strokes her hair as she drifts to sleep. "Ok, Jazz. Sleep well."

Dumb

Jazz's head throbs. She barely slept all night. She woke to lights out and the sounds of Tessa sleeping in an adjacent bunk. Still wrapped in a blanket in her stained dress, Jazz's frown refuses to budge as she stares at the space near her bed where Adrian had sat.

Her heart expands at the thought of him. *He's so special. What a guy.*

She showers after waking, even though it's the earliest of the hours. The thought of spending another moment in that dress sickens her. Once she returns to her room, she tosses and turns, regretfully not a moment more of sleep. She thought of Myra and Taz and where they might have gone. Would they be mixed up in a troubled situation like DJ put everyone in? Had she already run from situations like that? The thoughts make Jazz shudder.

She busies herself with thoughts of numbers and business structures. When the sun rises, she leaps out of bed and hurries down the hall.

Eddy walks into the shelter, gym bag slung over his shoulder. "You're up early."

Jazz stops her pacing. "I didn't sleep much."

Eddy nods. "I don't sleep at the best of times. Last night was a doozy."

"When I can't sleep, I think about business plans," Jazz blurts.

"Counting coins instead of sheep?" Eddy jokes.

"Adrian can't read," she says bluntly.

Eddy's brow furrows. "Yeah, I know."

"Should he really be in charge of the money then?"

"He can count," Eddy says in a low tone. "Are you trying to blame him for the lack of funding?"

"No. No, I—"

"—He's not dumb."

"I know that," she rushes. "He isn't. It was just a shock. I've never met anyone with a lack of education before."

"News flash; you've spent days around people like that."

"Wow, I really do live in a bubble," Jazz says, growing angry at herself. "Can I blame this on lack of sleep?"

Eddy grins. "Sure, I'll give ya a pass."

Jazz rubs her lips together, knowing she should leave the conversation be, but there is just one more question that is bothering her. "Hey, you said you're from Province, right?"

"Yeah?"

"That's an exclusive area. That would mean you have money? Why don't you back the site?"

"I have," he says flatly. "I got this site."

Jazz's mouth falls open. She blinks, trying to continue the conversation, but her words betray her.

"I've got to get ready for the day," Eddy says, passing by her. "You'll be ok."

She nods as Eddy paces towards his office. Her stomach clenches with a sense of dread. She resumes pacing the hall to steady her thoughts.

On her second lap, Jazz slows by Adrian's door. *Will he be up yet?*

Before another moment's thought, Adrian's door opens. He greets her with a growing smile.

"Hey there, do you need something?" he asks.

Jazz stares at the sunlight dazzling in his brown eyes, and says the message from her heart. "Just to see you."

Adrian's steps out of the doorway. "You want to come in?"

She grins as she slips inside.

Adrian closes the door behind them and sits down on his unmade bed. Without hesitation, Jazz sits beside him.

"How did you sleep?" he asks.

"I didn't."

His shoulders droop. "Oh no, really?"

"Yeah. I woke up some time after you left and tossed and turned."

"I didn't sleep either," he sighs. "Too bad. We could have stayed up talking to pass the time."

"That would have been nice instead of grappling with my thoughts."

"What's bugging you?"

"Oh, just everything and anything." She rubs his forearm. "Were you thinking about DJ?"

"Yeah, thinking I could have done more," he answers. "The boys were having issues together. I did nothing about it. I didn't take it seriously."

"You couldn't have predicted this."

"I should have talked to him more."

"What about the way I spoke to him?" Jazz replies. "I feel so bad. I was so rude to him."

"You just got here. You were still adjusting."

"I was being a spoilt brat," Jazz says, the corners of her lips curling. "It's ok, you can say it."

A hint of laughter escapes him. "I wouldn't put it that way, exactly."

"Many people who have known me my whole life call me that."

Adrian's face screws up. "Really?"

Jazz nods. "I dunno. Maybe they're right."

Adrian cups her hand. "You weren't spoilt last night. You were brave. Not to mention how generous you were with Myra. I wouldn't call you spoilt at all."

Jazz's blushes as her heart flutters, and a giggle escapes her. "Thanks. Brave is the best compliment I could ask for. You were so fearless in the dining room."

"Glad it came across that way, because I wasn't completely fearless."

"You do so much for the people here." She interlaces her fingers with his. "We need to save this place."

Adrian smiles. "I'm glad you still want to save it. I thought last night might have put you off."

"DJ was scary, but not enough to forget everything you shared with me. All of last night combined makes me hungrier to help."

"Speaking of hungry," Adrian says, standing, "want to get breakfast?"

Jazz stands and taps her empty belly. "Please."

Memory

Adrian can't stop smiling every moment he steals a glance at Jazz. Her doe eyes dip their gaze, subtly looking back at him.

A twinge of guilt hurts his stomach as his urge to flirt with Jazz takes precedence over lifting the mood in the dining room. Last night shook the few remaining people living in the shelter. Many haven't surfaced from their rooms, and Adrian wonders if some left during the night.

Jazz takes her plate to a table and Adrian's heart tugs for him to follow. He sits opposite her and mimics her smile.

"Maybe we could continue our conversation from last night?" Jazz suggests, a brow arching. "You know, the one we were in the middle of before all the craziness happened."

Adrian hugs his middle, forcing himself to stay seated despite his deep need to jump on the table and cheer. "Yeah, I'd like that."

Jazz nods at his plate. "Hungry?"

Adrian picks up a piece of toast and says, "I think so, but I don't think my appetite has come back to tell me to eat."

"Tell me about it," Jazz says. "I have to remind myself to eat, too.”

“What was that last night?” Gene asks, sliding a plate on the table and taking the seat by Jazz. “I didn’t know DJ was such a psycho.”

“He’s not a psycho,” Adrian is quick to say.

“*No*,” Gene replies sarcastically. “Sane people always threaten people with knives.”

“He hasn’t had an easy life,” Adrian counters, his heart pounding against his ribs.

“Gene,” Jazz whispers, “try to be a little more sensitive.”

“Hey, I can be sensitive,” Gene says, pointing to his chest, “but how would you feel if your roommate tried to kill someone or himself? Imagine if he had done that when we were all in bed.”

Adrian rubs his hands over his face and sighs. “I know.” Adrian lowers his hand and sees Jazz’s hand reaching across the table to him. He takes her hand and his chest eases.

Gene looks back and forth at the pair, and then his jaw drops. “Wait a minute, how’d it go last night?” He points to their clasped hands. “Good, I’m guessing.”

Their hands break apart and they both mutter, “Gene.”

“What?” Gene squeaks. “You know I had my fingers crossed for you guys. Look how cute you two are together.”

Heat lines the sides of Adrian’s face, and he laughs when he sees rose spread across Jazz’s cheeks.

Jazz cups a hand over her eyebrow. “Don’t laugh at me.”

“Yep, too cute,” Gene says, pleased with himself.

Adrian balls up a napkin and throws it at Gene. “Can you stop watching us, please?”

Gene bats the balled up paper away. “*Eww*.”

Adrian laughs. “I didn’t use it.”

Jazz snaps her fingers at Gene. “Max and Ferg want you.”

Gene rolls his eyes. “No, they don’t.”

Jazz points over Adrian’s shoulder. “Yes, they do.”

Adrian turns in his seat to see Max and Ferg waving.

Gene groans and pulls himself up from his seat, lifting his plate and moving to the next table.

"They were just waving," Jazz whispers, leaning in close. "But he was being a pest."

Adrian laughs. "You are so smart."

Jazz flicks her hair, grins showing off her pearly white teeth, and laughs cheekily.

For a moment everything grows quiet, with Adrian's heartbeat being the only thing he can hear clearly. He sits back in his seat, and says frankly, "I can't believe you're here."

She looks at him with confusion. "What do you mean?"

"What are the odds someone like you would wind up here?" He sits up, smoothing his hair back. "The way this city works, we should never have met."

Jazz bites her lip and replies, "That would have been a real shame."

They stand at the same time and walk their plates into the kitchen.

"You've liked it here?" Adrian asks, bracing himself for the answer.

"I mean, I've slept on a better quality mattress before," she teases. "But I'm more than glad I've met everyone here. It has opened my eyes."

"And you'll go fight for your father's company?"

Jazz leans against a bench, tilting her gaze to the ceiling. "All I want is to make my father proud."

"Every kid wants to impress their parents."

"You felt like that?" Jazz asks, pushing off the bench. "With what your parents did? You said they took you with them?"

Adrian nods. "Yeah. They sent me through windows, and into crawl spaces and safes."

"That's horrible."

Adrian shrugs. "I didn't exactly know any different. I didn't know those things actually belonged to people."

"What?" Jazz asks, her eyes bulging. "You were in people's homes."

Adrian hugs his waist, his shoulders falling forward. "I was just a kid and we lived in this run-down little house in The Limits. These were big mansions over on Sovereign Hill. I thought they were museums or shops or something."

"Your parents never explained it?"

"No. Social workers did later on."

"So the guilt came after they died?" Jazz says it more like a statement than a question.

"I did feel bad," Adrian says, looking into her eyes. "I do feel bad."

"You're doing more than your fair share to make amends. No one can say you don't care."

"Thanks."

"I'm still so sorry that you had to witness their death. No child should have to go through that."

An ache tears through the pit of his stomach. "I don't know if they started getting more reckless, or leaving behind too much evidence, but they were being tracked by the cops." Sickness dominates his insides. He swallows hard before continuing. "The only thing I remember feeling around them is panic."

Jazz touches his hand. "That's no way for a child to grow up."

His smile is limp. "That's why it's so important for me to help everyone who walks through our doors."

"But you can't feel responsible for everyone. It wasn't your fault they put you in those situations."

"I'm the last one left of my family. I have to make up for the shit they did." He cups her hand. "I got good at it. I'm not innocent."

Her eyes narrow. "Good at stealing?"

He nods, lips turning downward.

"Like you took initiative to steal?"

"You got good at your family business to impress your parents. I wanted to do the same thing. It was all I knew."

Jazz shifts away. "What did you do?"

"My parents were addicted to heists. I wanted to come into my own. When we did a string of hits through Sovereign Hill, I asked around which items made the most on the black market and were easiest to sell."

"Sovereign Hill was your target?"

Adrian shrugs, chewing his lip. "The people who could afford to lose something. They shouldn't be able to be so wealthy when the rest of us live on nothing."

"That doesn't give you the right to take it away." Jazz's eyes widen. "This is when you were a child?"

He nods, wary.

Her face sharpens with contempt. "You went to a large white home with pillars and a high brass gate?"

"Probably."

Jazz's eyes bulge and shine as her head shakes. "You went into a young girl's bedroom and took the things most precious to her."

Adrian falters, his heart palpitating. "Wait, what?"

Jazz stands tall, stomping a foot. "You stole a necklace. A silver locket with a blue stone."

"I... I..."

"You're the reason I don't have it!" Jazz yells.

"I don't—"

"—It was my mother's," Jazz wails, slamming a hand over her heart. "You stole my mother's memory."

Adrian raises his hand, wanting to reason with her. "Yes, jewellery is easy to get rid of, but..."

"Those things were all I had left of her!" Jazz spins and darts into the dining room.

"Jazz!" Adrian calls out.

He runs into the hall, but she's too fast, pulling open the front door and slamming it behind her.

"What's happened?" Gene's voice sounds behind him.

"I don't know," Adrian whispers.

"Jazz left?"

Adrian scrunches handfuls of his hair. "I've screwed up."

"But you need her. This place needs her."

"I don't have the whole picture. I don't know how I'd ever start apologising."

Gene steps in front of him, his face paler than usual. "What happens to this place without her?"

Adrian turns away, moving towards his office, his stomach churning. "Nothing. We're exactly in the same shit we've always been in."

Judgement

Jazz reefs open the front door and hits the cement outside. She looks back until she remembers she has no belongings to take with her. Her soiled dress is inside, but the idea of it sends her into a rage. Her hands ball into fists, her nails pierce her palms, and she lets out a shrill scream. She screams long and loud, scratching her throat and lighting a fire in her chest.

My mother. He stole my mother.

The locket she'd kept from memory for so long dangles from a chain in her mind. The image sends hot tears surging down her face.

She swipes at her face as she runs. A thought emerges from the back of her mind. *How do I get home?* She doesn't have any money. She doesn't have a phone to order a driver. Her pace slows as she looks over her shoulder. Someone back there would help her. She wished she'd gone out the back to find Hector, but the thought of running into Adrian keeps her moving away from the shelter.

Why was I so stupid? It was foolish to dream of romance. It affects logic, clouds judgement, and takes your eyes off the prize. Jazz hurries to the bus stop on the corner, pledging to return her full focus on securing the CEOship. It is time to put her efforts back into her business plan, completing her spreadsheets, and the presentation to the board.

She edges around a woman to read the bus timetable, when the woman pushes her and snaps, "Watch it!"

Jazz gasps as she regains her footing. She dusts her shirt. "Excuse me?"

The woman eyes her with disgust. "Don't even try sneaking on this bus. I saw you come from that alley. You people can't be trusted."

Jazz's mouth hangs ajar. She looks down at her donated clothes. Surely, she doesn't appear homeless or dirty. *Because I left the shelter she assumes I'm mistrustful?*

"Get out of here!" the woman snaps.

"I'm just trying to get home," Jazz says, voice shaky.

"I bet you don't have money for a ticket. Go somewhere and clean your face too. Horrible girl."

Jazz touches her cheek, wiping the remnants of tears. She backs away with fear the woman will hit her if she doesn't.

Jazz hurries along the sidewalk, realising she's heading into the Nightclub District. *Duh.* She slaps her forehead, moving toward the taxi stand. She hails a taxi. Once she's home, she can get some cash from inside. *Should have gotten out of here days ago.* Loathing boils inside of her to dangerous levels.

Blessing

Ethan wraps a towel around his waist, leaving the shower, and makes his way into the living room where his freshly brewed coffee awaits. He sits on the couch and kicks his feet on the table as he unlocks Jazz's phone and opens her emails. It's almost identical to her text messages. Multiples sent from Darius, questioning her whereabouts and why she hasn't checked in.

Ethan clicks his tongue as Darius enters his mind. He is yet to seal the deal in naming Ethan as his successor. Darius is still hoping his daughter will turn herself around and be the perfect face of Ultimate ME he raised her to be.

There is only one thing to do. Ethan has to take Jazz out of the running so he can gain all of Darius' attention.

Ethan opens an email and hits reply:

Father,

I'm sorry for being so absent. The cruise did me a lot of good and helped put things into perspective. But I wasn't fully honest with you. I left because I needed to think. Ethan proposed to me and I was having a hard time knowing whether to accept. But now I have come to a conclusion. I will marry Ethan and work beside him at Ultimate ME. Please, name him CEO and I will stand behind him. We can use his power and my name, and the company will be unstoppable in the industry.

Please don't worry about me, I am fine. I will return to Maiden City soon. I need to see Ethan.

Your daughter,

Jazz

Once Ethan clicks send, he retrieves the ring box from the counter. He opens up the box and light dazzles against the diamond engagement ring. He angles the phone's camera and snaps a picture.

Ethan walks into Darius' office, which he has come to think of as his own, and almost stumbles when he sees Darius behind the desk.

"You're back?" Ethan asks, not meaning to sound shocked.

"It was a mild heart episode," Darius grumbles, tapping at his keyboard. "Nothing that should keep me away from my work. It's not like I had a daughter by my bedside."

Ethan takes a sheepish approach, lacing his hands behind his back and edging his way into the office. "Speaking of, did she call you this morning?"

Darius grunts to himself. Ethan stops mid-step, waiting for his response. "No," Darius says.

Ethan continues towards the desk. "Oh, she said she would be, because..."

Darius sighs and stops typing. He glances up at Ethan and says, "She emailed me."

Ethan stays with the timid routine, widening his eyes and pointing to himself. "About me?"

Darius narrows his eyes. "She called you?"

"We had a lot to discuss."

Darius rests his palms on the desk and takes in a lengthy breath. "I don't understand why she didn't come to me right away. This decision affects all of us. If you two are planning to marry to run the company, I need to know these things."

"I know," Ethan says, lowering to an armchair. "She made me promise not to say anything. In hindsight, it was a bad decision, but I wanted to respect her wishes. I'm sorry I took my anger out on you the other day. It was misplaced. It also hurt me that Jazz left."

Darius lightens his expression and nods at Ethan. "Of course, you put your heart out on the line for a woman and she leaves on a party yacht."

"That isn't a deterrent, Darius. Believe me, I still want to marry your daughter." He finds his eyes. "I have your blessing?"

Darius takes him in, his mind crunching. "If you can bring her home and tame her childish ways, I'd be overjoyed to have you as a son-in-law."

Ethan grins. "Thank you, Sir."

"It will be my pleasure to officially welcome you into the Abadi family."

Ethan takes in his mentor. The colour has returned to Darius' face. He has overpowered his illness and remains the strong mentor Ethan always admired. Ethan's idolisation increases and he fidgets in his seat, buzzing for the moment he is named heir and told by Darius how proud of him he is.

"I will help guide her. Help her become more mature and conduct herself appropriately," Ethan says. "Lord knows after the scene she made in the bar she could use some help with decorum. Once we are married it will be easier to keep watch of her. I'd be doing it for your sake just as much as hers. You don't need the stress. Look at what happened by her leaving. Jazz will have a stake in the company, but she's too much of a loose cannon to hold the reins. You put too much into this company to have her tear it down. I'll be the Abadi to take the company to a higher level. I foresee takeovers and expansion. Ultimate ME will be bigger and better than ever before."

Darius smiles, a light dancing in his eyes. He holds out his hand, and Ethan takes it. They shake and Darius says, "I like the sound of that."

Enough

Adrian dashes into Eddy's office. "I've gotta talk with you. Jazz freaked out and left."

Eddy stands by his desk, phone to his ear, and panic on his face. "Do you know where Gene lives?"

"What? No. Why?"

"He's gone," Eddy blurts. "The caseworkers took him."

Adrian falls back on a chair. "But he was just here."

"They came back, and he willingly left." Eddy blows out a breath in frustration. He pulls back his dark blonde hair and shakes his head. "Why would he do that?"

"Maybe this place scared him?" Adrian wonders out loud, thinking over the last twenty-four hours. "Enough to go back?"

Eddy slams his desk. "You saw his face. We can't let him go back there."

Adrian stands and moves closer to his friend. "DJ wasn't your fault. Don't torture yourself."

Eddy gulps and shivers. "You didn't hear the things he said in session. Thinking over everything, I should have caught on."

“Ed, don’t.”

“We need to find Gene.”

“You’re right. We can’t let him go right back home to abuse. But how do we find him?”

“I dunno. I feel useless.” Eddy looks at him sideways. “You said Jazz left?”

“Mhmm.”

“Why?”

“I told her about my past.”

“That can’t be it.”

“She said something about her mother.”

“Her mother?”

“That I stole her memory.”

Boys

"**Gene**, you're alive," his mother bawls, dragging him into her arms at the front doorway of their home. "I was so worried. Where did you go?"

"I didn't mean to worry you," Gene says, pulling out of the hug. He looks past his mother to his father, who keeps his anger in check for the caseworkers benefit. "Hi Dad."

His father nods. "Gene."

"Is everyone ok?" Miss Eden asks from the front step, glancing at her watch.

"Of course," his mother cheers, briskly rubbing Gene's arms. "We have our boy back."

"We can give you some space to talk things through," Mr Duban says, nodding to Gene's father.

"Good," his father says, gesturing to Gene to come further into the house. "Get inside."

Gene's blood runs cold. His mother pats his back and pushes him towards the living room. He walks in, keeping his father in the corner of his eye.

When Gene sits on the worn, floral sofa, his father leans over him and wags a finger in his face. "No more funny business from you. You hear me?"

"Funny business?" Gene asks, sinking into the sofa.

"Don't play games with me," his father growls. "You are to come back into this house and act normal."

"*Normal?*" Gene scampers back on the sofa and turns to his mother, hoping she will remove the dread twisting his insides.

She sits beside him and pats his knee. "Just be like the other boys."

"What other boys?" Gene asks in a whisper.

His father grabs his collar and yanks him forward. "Don't back talk. You will be quiet and respectful, and you won't let any more disgusting vile things out of your mouth."

"All I said was, *I am gay.*"

Smack.

Gene's head hits the backrest after his father's hand whacks his face. Gene slides his hand over the throbbing wound as his mouth hangs open.

He turns to his mother, whose eyes are brimming with tears. "Mum?"

"Be a good boy," she pleads through sobs.

"I am," he replies, sitting up. "Why do I have to live a lie to live here? I don't want to have to wait until I'm eighteen to be me. Please, don't make me hide, or they'll send me to foster care."

His mother's eyes shift to his father and then back to Gene, expression unchanged.

Gene brushes back her hair. "Remember all the fun times we had when I did your makeovers? I'll still be the same boy."

His father shoves him, looming over him to say, "No more sissy stuff. You will act like a man."

Tears fill Gene's eyes as he looks to his mother.

His mother's face is streaked with tears, and she nods with a warbling throat.

"No, Mum..."

"You will do as I say!" his father yells.

"Please," his mother whispers. "Please be good. I have to stick by my husband."

Gene's stomach drops and his heart pounds to a slow beat. A shine to his mother's eyes says she wants to keep him, but the fear fogging her eyes confirms she's trapped. Gene grows sick, knowing his mother needs as much help as he does. But maybe if he leaves, his father won't hit her.

Gene stands and his father steps back, hatred burning in his eyes.

"Goodbye," Gene murmurs.

"What?" his mother wails.

His father flexes his arms and grits his jaw. "What?"

Gene wipes his face and takes them both in one last time, and then bolts for the front door.

"Don't you even think about coming back here!" his father yells. "We're through!"

Gene dodges the social workers as he races to the footpath. They call out to him, but he quickens his pace, dodging potholes and pedestrians as his thoughts struggle to keep up with him.

He catches his breath a few blocks away from his house, bending over and resting on his thighs. His heart cries to return to the shelter, but he reminds himself of the mess left behind when Jazz abruptly walked out on them. *Maybe if I make things right between Adrian and Jazz, he will let me stay with him. I'm the reason they fought, so maybe I can make them happy again.*

Gene pulls out his phone as he works on a plan. He opens Collage and taps on a trending post at the top of the feed. His jaw almost unhinges as he takes in the image and the ungodly caption.

"What the hell?" he yelps.

Destroyed

Jazz pays the driver and retreats into the Abadi Mansion. She forces the heavy front door closed and slams her back against it. Her heart shatters and her tears stream as her mother's locket swings in her mind. Thoughts of her mother tumble into overdrive.

She slaps her heart and tells herself to snap out of it. *Focus on what's important, you stupid girl.*

She dries her face and calls out to her father, stepping through the first floor of the mansion while gazing up at the dual winding staircase to the second floor.

"Father?" she tries again. The house is quiet. Too quiet. *Eerie.* Not even a housekeeper in sight. *Where is everyone?*

She stops outside her father's study and knocks on the door. "Father?"

The door creaks open. "Father?" Jazz peers inside. It's void of natural sunlight with no one inside.

Jazz creeps inside, looking over her shoulder, still unconvinced she's alone in the house. She tiptoes around the desk and pans the papers laying on top. She slides a few documents across the desktop and flicks her fingers between the pages of a folder.

Something in here will give me an edge at the board meeting. She wills something to magically appear in front of her and be the key to her success.

She sits on the desk chair and opens the drawer by her legs. She twists her lips, knowing the good stuff would be at the office. She slams the drawers closed and huffs. Something catches her eye by the computer keyboard. She tugs at the paper, examines the header, identifying it as an invoice from Maiden City University Hospital.

Hospital? Jazz's mouth falls open as she reads the notes about her father's recent hospital stay. *Why didn't he tell me?* She then purses her lips and shakes her head. *How could he? I hid purposefully.*

She slouches in the chair as the guilt slithers out of her stomach and takes hold of her body. *I could have used a phone at the shelter. I could have told him I was ok.* She rests her face in her hand as she wonders whether her disappearance caused his condition to worsen.

She sighs and rubs the puffiness under her eyes. She asks herself what she really wants to put forward to the board. How can she really make a difference? She thinks of young Gene with the sparkling brown eyes full of hope and the ugly bruise afflicting his sweet face. A sour taste lines the back of her throat. She never asked him how he got the bruise. But she wanted to know. She wanted to talk to him and help him. Her knuckles crack at the thought of Tessa and her job interview. She never bothered to coach her before she left, even though she could spot in an instant she would fail.

And Adrian.

A good man, she had called him. That is him now. What he did to her was in their childhoods. The locket swings from a chain in her mind, the blue stone shining and bouncing light. She grits her teeth and her stomach knots. *Why the locket?* She remembers it being a big robbery. Many things were taken, but the locket broke her heart.

She stands from the desk and paces out of the study, across the herringbone floor, and jogs up the staircase to the second floor. She opens the door to her expansive bedroom. The cream walls, plush white carpet, and the oak four-poster bed adorned with delicate opaque white fabric dancing in the breeze, sends a chill to her skin. Her wealth is grotesque. She spent four nights on a lumpy bunk bed mattress, and it was enough. With the surrounding community, there was no need for complaint.

She shakes off the new wave of guilt and moves to the shelf to the left of the desk. As a child, these shelves were a blush pink and filled with trinkets, toys, and picture books. Now they're cream and stacked with academic textbooks and progress reports from the gym she manages.

She perches on the edge of the bed and stares at the shelves. She closes her eyes and focuses on imagining what they looked like in her childhood. She sees the photographs of her and her father and the portrait of her mother before she was pregnant with her. Her mind pans across the silver jewellery boxes and the hand-sewn teddy bears. A memory resurfaces of the locket in her hands. Her small hands open the locket. Her heart races as her mind reveals the contents of the locket. The raven lock of her mother's hair. The only part of her mother she ever touched.

Stolen.

The last piece of her mother taken away from her. The moment that destroyed her childhood and forced her on the path of business over emotions. Spreadsheets over romance. A way no one could ever cause her that kind of pain again.

She opens her eyes and flings herself backwards on the cashmere comforter. The boy responsible is now the man who opened her heart to the possibility of romance. Her body tenses from the top of her skull down to her biggest toe. Adrian's face appears in front of her and she tilts her face to take in his features. He made her feel better about herself. Opened her eyes to bigger possibilities. Ways she could use her education and experience to a better use.

But could she trust him?

She rises from the bed, unable to decide what to do with the mess in her head. She walks into her marble-tiled bathroom. The only thing she's sure about is she needs a shower and to dress in something from her own wardrobe.

Illusion

Gene uses the map on his phone and lands at the entrance of Ultimate ME Head Quarters. He slips his phone into his pocket, inhales bravery, and walks into the lobby.

"Hold up," a man in all black with an earpiece tucked around his right ear, says, pushing Gene backwards. "Where do you think you're going?"

"I just..."

The security guard looks Gene up and down, smirking. "I don't think so."

Gene takes in his scruffy attire. *Fair enough.*

Gene backs away and darts out the front glass doors. He moves to the side of the building, dropping to the ground and unzipping his backpack. He would need to look the part in order to sneak in. He pulls out a silk scarf, hair products, black square sunglasses, and a fitted ash denim jacket.

He works product through his hair, watching through the phone's camera he propped against the steps. He takes a makeup wipe from the front pocket of his bag and swipes it across his face. Under his eyes, get three wipes. On closer inspection of his pores, he *eews* his reflection. He slings the scarf around his neck and ties it delicately at the front. He props the jacket on his shoulder and fits the sunglasses on the bridge of the nose, giving the illusion they may tip and provide someone the privilege of looking into his eyes.

He blows a kiss at his reflection and then slips the phone into his pocket. He stashes his backpack behind a dumpster and dusts his pant legs. He tilts his chin up and angles his shoulders back as he swans into the lobby. He reaches the elevator and peers over his shoulder, checking security is still in the building. The guard from earlier stands tall by the reception desk, hands clasped to his front and staring ahead.

The doors open, and Gene steps inside with cool confidence and hits the button for the top floor. The elevator doors close and his exhale blows like a mighty wind. *Phew.*

The doors ping open, and Gene steps onto the floor like he's meant to be there. He dips his sunglasses and eyes the secretary.

"Hey babe," he sing-songs as he swishes his hips her way. He twirls the jacket with a flick of his wrist and drapes it over his forearm. "Almost knock off time? I'm just here to see the big guy."

The mousy secretary's shoulders droop as she scans her calendar. "I have no more meetings scheduled. You are?"

Gene plants a palm on her desk and juts a hip, smiling. "Boy, I love your highlights. Where did you get them done?"

The secretary scrunches her hair with confusion. "I don't have highlights."

Gene clutches his chest, feigning shock. "You're kidding me. It's gorgeous." He bounces from the desk and skips to her side. "If you tell me it's natural, I'll just drop dead right here."

The secretary giggles nervously. "I've never dyed my hair."

"Oh my goodness," Gene gasps, running a hand through her hair. He smiles, thinking back on how easy it was to get in Holly's good graces. "I'm literally dying. You have to let me style it." He moves to face her. "That's why I'm here. I'm a stylist. I have a meeting with Mr Abadi because I'm supposed to start work on some models for the next campaign. Are you telling me he hasn't got my appointment scheduled?"

"Unless it's a mix up from when Mr Roth took over?" she suggests.

"Come again?"

The elevator pings open.

"Here he is now," the secretary says, gesturing to the man walking off the elevator. Gene already knows who he is from Collage. *Ethan Roth*. Jazz's competition.

"Mr Roth," the secretary says, "this is the stylist for the next campaign." She gestures to Gene, looking lost. "Sorry, your name again?"

"Yes, I'd love to know," Ethan says, removing a cufflink, "considering the CEO doesn't oversee the marketing campaigns."

The secretary's cheeks burn red, and she lowers her gaze to her keyboard.

"Ah, I need to talk to Mr Abadi," Gene says flatly.

Ethan cocks an eyebrow, looking Gene up and down. He nods at his office, removing his other cufflink. "Follow me."

Gene's courage gurgles to the pit of his stomach. His shoulders lock as he moves into the office behind Ethan.

"Shut the door," Ethan says, tossing the cufflinks on the desk and sliding off his jacket. "So, who are you really?"

Gene closes the door and mutters, "I... I..."

"It's easy to sweet talk Heather out there," he says, smiling to himself as he moves towards the floor-length mirror. "She might be one of the few women hired here not for her looks. Hmm, maybe I'll change that after they confirm my position at the board meeting tomorrow. Ha, maybe that can be Jazz's new job."

Gene touches his phone, remembering the post he saw when he

left his house. "You'd do that to your fiancé?"

Ethan's grin grows as he watches Gene. "You saw that, did you? She has a wealth of followers. She had to let it slip before the board meeting. It's all about the likes on the posts for that girl."

Gene slings his hands in his pockets as he walks further into the office. "Funny how she posted it without a phone."

Ethan's smile turns upside down. "Come again?"

"Jazz," Gene draws out. "She doesn't have her phone."

Ethan's hands sit on his hips. "And how do you know Jazz? I didn't take her for someone to hang out with twelve-year-olds."

Gene scoffs. "I'm not twelve." *What is with everyone saying that?*

Ethan opens a small cabinet, saying, "No matter how young you are, you do have style." Ethan pulls out two ties and holds them up for Gene. "Which should I go with?"

Gene puffs a laugh, wondering if he was serious. "I've seen that blue one in three of your latest posts. Go with the green."

Ethan returns the blue tie, and asks, "You're stalking me?"

"It's not hard to use Collage."

"I'm looking for another social media marketer," Ethan says, changing ties. "You interested?"

"Huh?" *Isn't that Jazz's job?*

Ethan moves towards Gene, giving him smouldering eyes and hypnotising him with his earthy cologne. "That is why you're here, isn't it? A job?"

"I need to speak with..." he trails off his sentence when Ethan's fingers dance down his back. "Hey, what are you doing?"

Ethan edges close to Gene's ear and tickles him with his breath. "You want a job, or looking for a sugar daddy?"

Gene wriggles away from Ethan and shoots his hands out in front of him. "Ok, I really need to speak with Mr Abadi."

"Mr Abadi is indisposed," Ethan says, walking towards Gene who continues to back away until he leans against the desk. "C'mon. Come work for me. It'll be fun."

Gene gulps as Ethan leans over him. "You know you have full on crazy in your eyes, right?"

Ethan straightens up and tilts his head, taking in Gene's vulnerable state. "You have three seconds to get out of here and stop wasting my time, or I'll make you regret it."

Gene pads his palm across the desk and slips a folder into his jacket, hoping it's something of use. He moves past Ethan, heart lodged in his throat, and bolts out of the doorway.

"If I see you back here," Ethan calls, holding his phone out towards Gene and hitting *snap*, "you won't be leaving!"

Gene taps the elevator down button frantically and almost trips over his own feet to get inside.

Ethan moves the phone to his ear, and says, "Ignacio, I'm sending you a picture. Track him."

Gene collapses against the back wall of the elevator as the doors close, his chest rising and falling in rapid succession.

Accept

Jazz pulls her ivory, silk robe tighter around her body as she ends her third unanswered phone call to her father. She tosses the cordless landline phone on her desk, wondering where he is if he's not at home or the office.

"Honey, I'm home," Ethan's voice enters her bedroom as he pushes the door open.

Jazz holds her robe close to her body as she whips around to him. "Ethan, what are you doing here?"

"Such a warm greeting, Miss Abadi." He waggles his phone in the air. "I get the security alerts since your father has taken ill."

"Where is he?" Jazz asks, taking a wide step forward. She adds in an anxious whisper, "He's not back in hospital is he?"

Ethan's eyebrows raise, and he smiles. "So you heard about that?"

Jazz *tsks* and rolls her eyes. "Where is he, Ethan?"

Ethan bats a hand, walking further into her bedroom. "He's fine, stop fretting." He looks around at her belongings, and his eyes land on the bed. "I've never been in here before. It's oddly exactly what I expected. Almost feminine with a consuming addiction to business."

Jazz's stomach quivers. "Get out of my bedroom."

"You want this back?" Ethan asks, pulling out her phone from his trouser pocket.

Jazz groans and snatches it from him. "What about the rest of my stuff? Credit cards?"

"I have your bag at the office," Ethan says, amused. "I know how much you can't live without your phone. I'm surprised you've gone this long. Look at you, you're already hooked."

Jazz taps her phone screen. "You've kept it charged?"

"I needed to take matters into my own hands."

"And what does that mean?"

"I didn't know when you'd resurface, and you never gave me an answer to my question, so I had to decide for you."

"What in the world?" Jazz murmurs, opening up Collage and taking in the bubble of hearts filling the page. She hits the newest post to enlarge it. A photo of a diamond ring sitting in a jewellery box. The tagline says, 'I said yes.' "What did you do?"

"Go along with it, Jazz," Ethan says, direct. "We need to move forward. The board meeting is tomorrow and we can't sit on our hands any more. They are at a standstill because I make good business sense, but Darius is being sentimental toward you. We need to put the board at ease and team up for a smooth transition."

"I will not sit in the shadows and let you destroy everything my father built."

Ethan groans, throwing his head backward. "I'm not looking to destroy anything."

"What about your parents' company? You've totally abandoned it!"

Ethan scowls and turns away from her. "They did that themselves."

"What are you talking about? You took over, and they retired to travel."

"Exactly!" he yells, hitting the wall with a fist. He glares at her, nostrils flaring. "They didn't care about losing the company. They moved on like it was nothing. Treating me like nothing, like they did my entire life. It is a pleasure stripping that company down to its parts and selling them off to the highest bidder."

"You're just going to do it again."

"I thought about it," Ethan says, cracking his neck from side-to-side. "But I respect your father. He's someone to admire and aspire to be like. I just don't need him around for that."

"What are you going to do to him?" Jazz asks, rushing toward him. "He has a heart condition. He can't deal with undue stress."

"Oh, I'm aware," Ethan says, and takes hold of her shoulders. "It's you I'm after."

She thrashes against his grip. "Let go of me."

"You spoilt little heiress," Ethan says, pushing her backwards onto the bed. He plants his palms, either side of her, on the comforter and looms over her. "You take for granted the life afforded to you. Do you know how hard the rest of us have to work to get what he gave you for free? Because of your name?" Ethan grabs her jaw, making sure she looks directly into his burning eyes. "Be damn sure I will take that name away from you."

"You're insane," Jazz says through his grip. "You can't force me to marry you."

"What happens to you when they name me successor?" Ethan says, panning his gaze down her chest and around her torso. "Are you doing all that study to stay a gym manager?"

"You heard my father, I'm promoted to senior management, regardless. And, hey, my face is up here."

Ethan laughs but moves his gaze back up to meet her eyes. "That's if your father is still around. His health is failing. I've already convinced him to step back and let me take over so he can concentrate on maintaining a positive quality of life."

"What have you done to him?"

"You need me, Jazz. Without me, you're out of the company." Ethan runs a hand down her bare thigh. "Isn't the company the only remnants of a family you have left? Do you really want to lose that?"

The hairs on the back of her neck stand up. A chill runs down her spine. Her mouth runs dry. Sweat coats her neckline. "Stop touching me."

"We have a deal?" he whispers, lowering himself to smell the perfume on the nape of her neck. "We can make us official?"

"If I say yes, will you get off me?"

A throaty laugh pours out of Ethan. His hand runs up the inside of her thigh and pinches her skin. "Why don't we test out married life right now?"

Jazz pushes the base of her palm into his chest in one powerful motion. Ethan splutters a cough and pushes off the bed. Jazz soars a knee into his gut to send him backwards.

Ethan lands onto the carpet with a thud.

Jazz pushes herself up and leans over to watch him get up. "Learn to keep your hands to yourself."

After two loud coughs, Ethan stands and dusts himself off. "I'll forgive you this one time for crushing a five-thousand dollar jacket."

"I know the day-to-day operations of our sites. Remember, I'm a certified personal trainer. Because I care about making the company the best it can be. I do the legwork to be the best *I* can be."

"Keep that spunk for the wedding night." He straightens his tie and winks. "I dig it."

Jazz retches. "Just get out."

Run

Gene's thoughts trip him up. As he runs, he thinks about creepy Ethan, Jazz's fake marriage, finding Adrian, and staying away from his father. The mess in his head keeps his eyes off the ground, and he trips over cracked concrete.

The late hours of the night darken his surroundings. His pace slows. *Where the heck is Adrian's shelter?* Gene spins in a circle. All the alleys look the same. Had he run too far?

"Police! Freeze!" an officer yells from the top of the alley.

Gene's heart leaps in his throat.

"Stop!" the officer calls.

Gene's knees knock. He already walked into HQ. He can't be followed for that. *It must be Ethan's phone call.* He knew not to trust Ethan. He runs, somehow knowing not to trust this cop.

With his backpack swishing on his back, Gene races through the streets of the Nightclub District. He picks up speed and the officer's shouts muffle.

He stops to take in his surroundings, trying to retrace his steps from the other night. The police officer gains on him, so he panics and dives behind a dumpster.

He frantically taps at his phone, but he has no idea what address to type in the map function.

"Oh, you've got to be kidding me!" a voice yells from above.

"Huh?" Gene spins in place, looking up.

The dark sunglasses, blonde hair, and bomber jacket look down on him from atop a fire escape ladder.

"Oh, hey." Gene says, puffing and waving.

"What are you doing back here?" she yells over the railing. "Didn't you go into the shelter?"

"Yeah. I'm trying to get back there."

She shoots an arm straight out in front of her. "Down that alley, hang a right, and then second alley on the left. Go!"

"Thanks," Gene yells, but quickly slaps his hand over his mouth when the police officer's voice sounds from a nearby alley.

The girl above retreats into her smelly hideout.

Gene's heart booms in his chest. He holds the straps of his backpack and runs to safety.

Ambush

Adrian trudges across the cracked cement, in the early hours of the morning, to the nearby St Andrew's church. The prospect of the shelter closing stabs at his gut. His neck is stiff from stress and his back gnarled in knots. He used all his money to float the shelter, but now there was nothing left. St Andrew's is his last hope. The people need a place to go.

With trepidation, he approaches a sister who recognises him, saying, "Adrian, hello. How are you?"

Adrian stops on the steps of the church, blowing out a breath and rubbing the back of his neck. "I'll level with you, not well. Any chance you can take anyone else in?"

The nun looks at him with surprise. "You're asking for yourself?"

He shakes his head. "No. We're falling apart over there and I don't think we can keep the centre running. The women and children? Just a few. If you could arrange something?"

The nun's face softens with a frown. "I'm sorry, dear. We aren't taking in any new people. The city is making it hard for all."

Adrian nods, moving down the steps. "I understand. Thanks,

anyway." He pauses on a step and asks, "Did you see a woman and a child? Dark skin. Mother wearing a red scarf over her hair."

The nun shakes her head. "No, sorry."

"That's ok. Thanks."

"Adrian," the nun calls out.

"Yeah?"

"We might be able to take a few."

An ounce of relief fills his lungs.

"A small few."

"Thank you, sister. That's a massive help."

The nun smiles, nods, and returns inside the church.

Adrian rubs the pain from his chest and sets off back to the shelter. He'd find younger women and tell them to go to the church before the nun changes her mind. He'll figure out something with the boys. He's banking on them being less vulnerable on the streets.

"Adrian!" a frantic voice calls out.

Adrian turns around in search of the voice and finds Gene racing towards him, arms flailing and face reddened.

"*Whoah, whoah,*" Adrian says, flashing his palms like stop signs. Gene skids to a halt in front of him, and he takes his arms and stands him upright. "Try to calm down. What are you doing back here? Where were you running from?"

Gene breathes in and out with fear consuming his actions. He rushes a few jumbled words until Adrian stops him.

"Hey, hey, catch your breath first. You're all right." Adrian wraps an arm around the kid. "I'm so glad you're back. I was sick with guilt that we'd sent you back to some horrible place and you were—"

"—Bigger fish!" Gene interrupts, throwing his arms up and stepping out of Adrian's embrace. "We need to help Jazz."

Adrian takes a step back, eyeing him sceptically. "What do you mean?"

"There's some sick, weird arranged marriage thing going on."

Adrian opens his mouth, about to ask Gene to explain, but then he remembers what Jazz shared with him. "Ethan."

"Yes," Gene cheers, patting Adrian's arm. "That creep. We need to get Jazz away from him."

Adrian folds his arms. "What do you know about him?"

"I met him last night." Gene shivers. "He thinks he's God's gift to men and women."

"He came on to you?"

"It was so gross." Gene grimaces. "He's super hot, but man, his insides are ugly."

"Wait," Adrian says, shaking his head, trying to catch up. "You met this guy? When? How?"

"Look, we don't have time," Gene says, shoving him into the shelter. "He's set up this whole engagement thing with Jazz and he's very intimidating. Two more minutes with him and I would have agreed to marry him."

Gene hurries Adrian into the common room and flicks on the TV. He scans the channels until he hits the news station. "See!" he says, pointing at the ticker scrolling at the bottom of the screen. "Ultimate ME board meeting today to decide new CEO. That's where Jazz is going."

Adrian is having a moment of déjà vu. "Oh," he whispers, almost in pain. He sits and points to the screen. "She had this moment of panic one day when we were in here. The TV was on, and they were talking about a company. It must have been this one. This is the one her father started?"

"Yes," Gene cheers, smacking his hands together. "You're on the ball now."

"Gene?" Eddy asks in surprise, walking into the room. "You're back? What happened?"

Gene backs away, waving his hands. "No time to catch up, Ed. Adrian and I need to go."

"Go?" Eddy asks. "Go where?"

"Jazz is in trouble," Adrian whispers, feeling like he has no energy as the guilt grounds him to the earth.

"Say it with a little more passion," Gene says, and then fills Eddy in on what happened when he met Ethan. He then pulls out his phone to the Collage post of the engagement ring. "She didn't do this. He did."

"Adrian," Eddy says, rising panic shaking his voice.

"I also got this," Gene says, pulling out a folder from his backpack. "I don't know what it means, but Ethan had it on his desk, and I'm hoping it can help Jazz."

Adrian waves off the folder when Gene holds it out to him.

Eddy takes the folder and asks, "Why were you at Ultimate ME?"

"I saw the Collage post and wanted to tell Mr Abadi it was fake," Gene says. "I made Jazz and Adrian fight when I arrived and recognised Jazz. I wanted to help make things better." He looks to Adrian. "Sorry."

Adrian sighs. "Genie, you're not the reason Jazz left. You're not to blame."

Eddy's eyes widen as he scans the first page of the document. "It's a list of phone numbers of the top political figures and heads of corporations in Maiden City." He flips to another page. "There's more numbers and dollar amounts. Like minimum bribery amounts?"

"Bribery?" Adrian questions. "So the government is just as slimy as corporations?" *I can't take that grant money.*

Eddy lowers the folder. "I knew this city was messed up, but I didn't know the corruption was this organised."

"Is Jazz's father on that list?" Gene asks. "Jazz is so organised. Does she get it from him?"

"Jazz wouldn't be on that list," Adrian counters. He swallows and folds his arms across his mid-section. "Is she?"

"She's not," Eddy replies quickly.

"So Ethan is paying people off to get the company for himself?"

Gene asks.

"Looks that way," Eddy says. He turns another page, and something falls out of the back of the folder. "What was that?"

Adrian scoops it up. It's a photo of Jazz. The angle and blur of the image show someone snapped the photo in a hurry.

He shows it to Eddy. "It doesn't look like she knew this was being taken."

Eddy squints at the photo, and then hurriedly turns to the back of the folder. "Man, there are heaps of them."

"He's having her followed?" Gene asks anxiously.

Eddy reads another piece of paper and Adrian reads his face for clues. Eddy meets his eyes. "It's a rehab admittance form. Jazz has a substance issue?"

"Hell no!" Gene blurts. "I follow everything about her. No way."

"She wouldn't," Adrian says, shaking her head. "You had a session with her?"

Eddy nods. "They're trying to silence her."

"She's going into an ambush," Adrian says, turning to the door. "We have to help her."

Gene pulls him back. "Not like that."

"What are you talking about?"

Gene gestures to his attire. "You'll never get in dressed like that. And that hair. You need to look the part."

"Oh, bull," Adrian scoffs.

Eddy nods to Adrian. "Listen to him on this one."

Adrian rolls his eyes and sighs. "Ok. What do you propose we do?"

Gene grimaces. "I'm gonna have to wade through that unholy mess of clothes again."

"There's nothing new in there," Adrian says.

"Is that bloodstain still on your shirt?"

"It's washed," Adrian says apprehensively. "You want me to wear it again?"

"It's emergency time," Gene says. "I need an iron and some thread. I'll work quickly."

Eddy passes the folder to Adrian. "You need to work at the snap of a finger to get there in time."

Approval

Ethan straightens his tie and winks at his reflection. He turns to the desk in Darius' office and asks his mentor, "Ready to go?"

"Just a minute."

"I trust you're feeling well after last night's spa treatment?"

"The hotel stay was a bit much. I could have rested in my own home."

"You don't appreciate my efforts?" *I know I slept better knowing where you were.*

Darius chuckles as his eyes scan the last page of Ethan's proposal to the board. "Of course, Son. Aren't you planning on walking into the boardroom with your fiancé?"

"She'll be here," Ethan says, checking the time on his phone. "You know Jazz, she likes to make a grand entrance. Or at least that's what we tell people to hide how scattered she is."

Darius looks to the window and shakes his head. "I thought I knew who she was."

"Don't be hard on yourself. It's human to see your daughter through rose-coloured glasses. I'm sorry she broke the spell at such an important time. I had hoped she'd keep in line to get us through this meeting."

"You're worried she'll embarrass you in front of the board?"

Ethan scratches his chin. "Maybe it would be best if she sits this one out. Is that what you are suggesting?"

Darius lifts the document and gestures it at Ethan. "Your plan details you and she work together. She needs to be in the room and show her face during the meeting. If she gets out of line and needs a time out, so be it."

Ethan chuckles and gestures to the door. "Shall we?"

Darius moves around the desk and hands the document to Ethan. "Good luck in there."

"Thank you, I appreciate it."

They move across the executive floor to the boardroom.

"Mr Roth," Mrs Salinger from the board says, greeting them by the frosted glass door. "Congratulations on the engagement. Where is your bride-to-be?"

"Thank you," Ethan says, taking her hand. "She'll be in soon."

"It was a surprise to hear about it," Mr Fryer says, taking his seat at the long narrow table.

"Well, you know Miss Abadi," Ethan says, placing his paperwork on the small table by the projector screen. "She must let the whole world know what's going on in her life. But it's also what makes her so valuable to our corporation. Her Collage account gives such a great return on investment. It's an impressive skill, just not a CEO-worthy skill."

Some mutters of laughter rise from the greying old men as they take their seats.

"But having Jazz in senior management is important to my future father-in-law." Ethan sends a smile Darius' way as Heather helps him into his chair. "And me. I want to be working side-by-side with my wife. We will be the new generation of the Abadi family to take the company to the next level. Sir, do you wish to add anything before I start my presentation?"

All eyes land on Darius.

Darius clears his throat, and his face brightens with a peaceful smile. "As most of you know, I had what could be described as a near-death experience. Ethan Roth has stayed by my side and helped me speed through my recovery. He is diligent, hard-working and extremely motivated. Ultimate ME will be in expert hands."

"So he has your approval?" Mr Fryer asks, clicking a pen. "You've named him your successor?"

Darius takes another look at Ethan, then returns to Mr Fryer. "Yes, he has my backing. The board still has the final say, of course, but I'm confident in Mr Roth."

Ethan rubs his hands together, grinning enthusiastically. "Shall we begin?"

Embrace

Jazz runs into the lobby of HQ, her sunny yellow skirt billowing around her legs and her stiletto heels clicking.

"Oh, Miss Abadi," the lobby receptionist says, walking by with a bundle of packages and a headset clipped over her hair. "How are you? Congratulations on your upcoming nuptials."

Jazz gags and forces a smile. "Thanks. Did you see my father arrive?"

The receptionist checks her watch. "He and Mr Roth should be in the boardroom now."

"*Damn.*" The elevator pings open. "Thanks." Jazz hastily moves inside and hits the button for the executive floor.

She steadies her breath on the way up. Conflicting ideas plague her head. Did she want to contest the CEOship? She rubbed her fragile heart. She needs to speak to her father. Ethan had him locked away somewhere last night. But surely he's in the boardroom. If Ethan wanted her there, he'd want her father there too.

"Father!" Jazz yells, bursting into the boardroom as Ethan is mid-sentence, pointing to a slide on the projector screen.

She pushes past Ethan and lands by her father's sides. She drops to the ground and clutches his hand. "Father, are you ok?"

Darius shifts in his chair, and a frown tightens his expression. "Now you decide to check in?"

"I... I didn't know..." she stammers.

"Miss Abadi," Mrs Salinger scowls. "That was a crude outburst. Not to mention you're late."

Jazz stands, eyeing Mrs Salinger with contempt. The only woman on the board. A woman concerned with decorum and acting 'lady-like.' A woman Jazz has never cared for.

"Jazz, why did you disappear?" her father asks. "I thought someone injured you, or kidnapped, or worse."

"But father, sometimes we can go days without..."

"Why would you be so reckless at a time that is so important to us and our company?" Darius questions. He glances at Ethan and back to her. "I've been informed of the alcohol issues that have arisen."

Gasps erupt from the board.

I should have known. She shoots Ethan a look, who has fake concern scribbled across his face.

"So now you're faking a substance abuse problem too?" she asks him, loud enough to engage every ear in the room.

Ethan slides a hand over his heart, his gaze softening as he edges toward her. "Jazz, I love you. I'm concerned about you. I want you to get the help you need. I want to be there with you every step of the way."

Jazz retches and then hisses a laugh. "You've got to be kidding me."

Mr Fryer stands from his seat. "Please, can you all please act with some professionalism and stick to the matter at hand?"

Jazz rolls her eyes and faces her father. "He had my phone and made the posts from my Collage account."

"What are you talking about?" Darius asks.

"Why are you being like this?" Ethan asks, gently cupping her wrist. He leans in and stage-whispers, "Is that liquor on your breath?"

As Mrs Salinger gasps like a woman in a 1950s film, Jazz reefs her arm from Ethan's grip, disgusted. "Don't you dare!"

Ethan steps past Jazz, saying to Darius, "I'm still committed to Jazz and getting her the help she needs." He looks across to the board members. "I'll stand by her whilst keeping the company afloat."

"He's a fraudster," Jazz accuses, sending her arm out pointed to Ethan as she finds her father's eyes. "He faked our engagement."

"What are you talking about?" Ethan asks, letting his frustration get the better of him. "You said yes. Did you decide to take it back after your booze-cruise?"

"Booze-cruise?" Jazz asks, screwing her face up.

"I was sceptical when Ethan first proposed the idea to me," Darius begins, calm and collected, "but perhaps, dear daughter, you should accept his marriage proposal."

"What?" Jazz's head feels seconds from imploding.

"You are obviously struggling to keep your mental state in check."

"Ok." Jazz closes her eyes and raises her hands. "I don't know what kind of rubbish he's been feeding you. How about I make my presentation and you can decide for yourself?"

"Mr Roth is still part way through his presentation," Mrs Salinger says.

Ethan smirks and steps away from the podium. "No, no. It's fine by me. Please, Jazz, take your place and make your speech."

Jazz takes a deep breath and moves behind the podium, ignoring Ethan's sneer. She takes in all the faces, and then says, "I don't want to be CEO."

Murmurs run up and down the table in questioning tones.

"I've spent the last few days at a refuge centre for vulnerable and homeless people. The work is rewarding, and for the first time, I've felt truly fulfilled. I'll concede the CEOship to Ethan with plans to personally fund the shelter. If anyone on the board wants to buy my shares, it would help my ability to financially support the work."

"STOP THIS," Darius bellows, standing for the first time. "I'm incredibly disappointed in your actions. I asked you to fight for your place at the top, not go running from it."

"I wasn't running," Jazz argues. "I needed time. Ethan ambushed me with a fake proposal and—"

"—Fake proposal?" Mr Fryer questions.

"You should have been stronger than to let Ethan rattle you," Darius fires back.

Jazz's heart pounds in her ears. "Did you... You knew Ethan would ask me to marry him?" Jazz asks, her voice going up an octave. "Why didn't you warn me?"

"I thought Ethan took on my advice. When I didn't give my blessing, I assumed I'd taken care of it and there was no need to notify you."

"But you still agreed to him taking over the company?"

"No. I told you. You needed to prove yourself. To be worthy of the title and be the embodiment of the Abadi name."

"And what about honouring my mother's name? Living courageously like she did."

The frosted glass doors burst open and over her shoulder, Jazz sees Adrian and Gene stumbling into the room.

"Adrian?" she questions. "What are you two doing here?"

"What is the meaning of this?" Mr Fryer shouts. "How did you get in here?"

"Jazz," Gene says, holding out a document folder. "You need this."

"Who are these people?" Darius asks, rubbing a fist against his heart. "Jazz, you know these two?"

"They are from the shelter I was staying at this week." She smiles at Adrian and Gene. "They can verify I wasn't living it up on a yacht out at sea."

"A yacht?" Adrian asks.

"Sounds a lot better than where you were," Gene remarks.

Adrian nods. "If Jazz needs someone to prove where she was, then we have a whole centre filled with people who got to know her over the last few days."

"You people," Mr Fryer says, standing and waggling his finger at Adrian and Gene. "Out at once! This boardroom is for authorised personnel only."

Jazz spots the offence in the boys' eyes and quickly motions for them to leave the room with her. She tells the board she will return after a moment and follows them out of the room.

"Why are you here?" Jazz questions them.

"I know I'm probably the last person you want to see," Adrian says, his posture slouched.

Jazz bats a hand, wanting to forget the ugliness that made her flee the shelter.

"But you need to see this," Gene says, handing her the document folder.

Jazz opens the folder and shakes her head. "This is Ethan's business plan. I've seen this. He showed it to me."

"No, look at the back pages," Gene urges.

Jazz flips through the pages and finds a log of items. She tilts her head as she inspects the papers, working out what exactly she's looking at. "A list of phone calls?" She examines the next page and sees a list of names of high-ranking city officials and law enforcement officers, their contact information and hand-written notes. *Are these the numbers the Mayor was talking about with Ethan?*

When she gets to the next page, she's taken by such immense surprise she drops the folder. The page with pictures of her by her bedroom window, leaving the gym, and walking into HQ, stare up at her from the floor.

"He's following me?" Jazz says in a hush, her hands shaking.

"He had some shady cop follow me through the streets," Gene tells.

"I didn't know he'd be this devious," Jazz says, sadness and anger brimming inside her.

"We figured there was more you didn't know about," Adrian says.

"You need to get this guy," Gene says. "Don't let him get away with this."

Jazz presses her hands into her stomach as it swishes inside of her. "I think I'm going to be sick."

Adrian moves in closer, slipping an arm around her back and holding her shoulder.

"It shouldn't surprise me," Jazz whispers. "Ethan is a pig."

"Creep," Gene mutters. "We saw the engagement post."

"Ethan had my phone all this time," Jazz says. She turns to find Adrian's eyes. "The post was a fake."

Adrian nods. "I know. You told me what this guy is like. I don't like the thought of you anywhere near him."

Jazz slips out of Adrian's embrace and puts on a brave smile. "I can handle myself." She runs her eyes along Adrian's attire, noting the stitching on the sleeve of the dress shirt. "You're getting used to dressing up?"

"Even with a bloodstain, it's still the nicest shirt in the shelter," Gene says, fixing Adrian's collar.

"Looks like you cleaned it up," Jazz says. "You're a fast worker, Gene."

"You need to get in there," Adrian says to Jazz, serious. "We just wanted you to have all the information."

Jazz looks at the papers by their feet. "How did you get these?"

Gene spins her back to the frosted boardroom doors. "Never mind that. Just show that clown who's boss."

Choice

Jazz slams her hands against the doors to push them open. She collected the images from the floor and holds them high.

She tosses the paper at Ethan. "What the hell is this?"

Ethan looks at the crumpled paper, his eyebrow arching. "I don't know. You tell me."

"You're having me followed," Jazz accuses.

"*Jazz,*" Darius hisses.

"Jazz, if I was having you followed," Ethan begins, "I would have brought you home. All I got from you was a text message saying you were on a boat."

Jazz groans, scratching her throat. "Stop lying!"

Ethan steps close to Jazz and pushes back a lock of her hair.

Jazz retches and flinches from his touch.

"We talked about this," Ethan whispers to feign intimacy, but loud enough for everyone to hear. "We will work through this together. Get you through your issues and work together at the helm." Ethan turns to Darius. "But maybe it's best I take control for the first few months as we get Jazz the help she needs."

Jazz pushes against Ethan's chest. "I'm not a drunk! Would you stop this?"

"Everyone saw the footage from Overity," Ethan says, gesturing to the board. "Please, Jazz, let me help you."

Jazz moves past him, to her father. "All I've done is study and work. When have you ever known me to go to a party or a bar that wasn't purely for work purposes?"

"We don't see a lot of each other," Darius says slowly. "Perhaps I missed something?"

"All I've done is to be loyal to you," Jazz whimpers, tears welling in her eyes.

Darius wipes a thumb under her eye. "Tears?"

Jazz sniffs and looks away. "I know, not professional."

"You disappeared, and my health declined," Darius says. "I let my vulnerability take in Ethan's every word. Who you really are didn't allow me to see sense. You're allowed to have emotions."

"You've never let me before," Jazz replies.

"Please," Darius says, gesturing to the door. "A moment outside. Board members, please indulge me in taking a private word with my daughter."

"This meeting has been most unorthodox," Mrs Salinger says, jaw clenched.

"Be quick," Mr Fryer adds.

Jazz and her father hurry into the hall.

"Those emails weren't from you?" Darius questions, his tone low.

"No, Father. I haven't had my phone since I was at the bar with Ethan. I didn't know he had it." Jazz's emotions get the better of her and her eyes fog with tears. "I didn't know you grew so ill. Please believe me. I would have been by your side otherwise."

Darius takes her hands firmly. "I kept the severity of my condition from you. Truth is, I'm on a timer. That's why I needed to rush the board meeting and name a successor. I didn't think you were ready yet, but I didn't have a choice."

Jazz moves into her father's arms and her voice quivers. "I wish you had told me."

"I'm sorry, sweetheart."

"Sweetheart?" Jazz repeats, head resting against her father's rising and falling chest. "You've never given me a pet name before."

Darius strokes her hair. "I should never have pulled away from you."

"I never wanted to upset you," Jazz says, her chest tightening. "I know you've always thought of me as the reason Mother died."

Darius' arms unravel and he moves back to meet Jazz's eyes. "That's not true."

Jazz wipes her wet cheeks. "Yes, it is."

"I've never blamed you. You've always felt this way?"

Jazz looks to his shiny brown shoes and nods.

Darius lifts her chin. "It wasn't your fault. You're my greatest triumph. I should have reached your mother sooner. If there's anyone to blame, it's me." He lets out a weighted sigh. "I should never have stopped talking about her."

Jazz grinds her teeth, scrunching her eyes closed as the pain in her heart intensifies.

Darius pulls her in close, and the slow beats of his heart ease her.

"You know these two?" Darius asks.

Jazz lifts her head and looks over her shoulder at Adrian and Gene. "Yes. When I blacked out after my night with Ethan, they helped me."

"I don't want you selling your shares. I want you to remain part of the company."

"What I'd really like is my gym."

"I thought you didn't want to run it anymore?"

"No, I want the site for the refuge centre. So we can house more people in a clean and modern environment."

Darius smirks and unravels his arms from around her. "You want our most lucrative site as a donation? Jazz, it's our number one site. That's why *you* run it. You are the best manager we have. I'm sorry, it's out of the question. We would never hand over that property. And the surrounding businesses would never allow homeless people living in the Business District. You know that."

Jazz frowns and nods, her eyes glancing back at Adrian.

Darius huffs and marches towards the boys. He looms over Adrian, and Jazz notices Gene squirm and gulp.

Darius holds a hand out to Adrian. "You've been helping my daughter?"

Adrian shakes Darius' hand and says, "With all due respect, Sir, Jazz doesn't need help. She's much too independent to take it, but she's more than generous to help us."

Darius turns to Jazz. "This is why you want the gym? To expand his business?"

"It's not a business," Jazz replies. "It's a not-for-profit. And yes, I want to help them. I want to do something worthwhile and honourable."

"Courageous," Darius says, "like your mother."

"They have money issues," Jazz says. "I need to help keep them afloat."

Darius beckons her to follow him back into the boardroom. "I have a decision to announce."

Ready

Ethan takes in a sharp breath as Darius re-enters the boardroom. His confidence wavers as Darius' eyes gleam with purpose.

"Ladies and gentleman of the board, I will not be stepping down as CEO of Ultimate ME," Darius announces.

"Father, no," Jazz says, tugging his arm. "Your heart."

"This is outrageous," Ethan blurts. "Sir, where is this coming from?"

"Jazz Abadi will step down from her position at the company. We will commence interviews to appoint her replacement." Darius nods to his daughter. "You can provide the board with names of staff members you feel are fit to take over management."

Apprehensively, Jazz nods and says, "Yes. I think Marcus would be the right fit. He had problems working with me, but with my absence, he'll allow the site to thrive."

"Hang on," Ethan begins, but almost stumbles over his own feet when Darius charges towards him.

Darius' eyes burn into him. "I am not handing over the company to a cheat and a liar."

Ethan's heart drops to the pit of his stomach. His chest constricts, and he finds taking his next breath a struggle.

"But you can't be abandoned again," Darius says in a softer tone. "You're fixated on your parents' treatment of you and it's turned you into this sneaky vindictive individual. You'll stay on under my supervision. If your attitude and business practices improve, I can consider you for succession again."

"Wait," Jazz says. "You're not seriously going to keep him on?"

"He'll only get worse if I let him go," Darius replies.

"Don't talk about me like I'm a pet project," Ethan snaps, heat rising from his collar.

"You need to learn some honesty and integrity," Darius says, and the look in his eyes sends a sharp pain in Ethan's back.

Mr Fryer stands and says, "So, we're done here?"

Darius nods his acknowledgement to the board, and they pack up their documents and leave the boardroom.

Ethan groans and stamps a foot. "Are you serious? You're taking all of this away from me?"

"I'm still mentoring you," Darius says gently. "You're not ready yet. I'll oversee your actions and sign off on all work before it becomes official."

Ethan's anger erupts inside him, and he storms out of the boardroom.

In the hall, he spots the boy who was in his office the evening before. "*You*. What are you doing back here?"

Ethan marches towards the boy, who utters panicked noises.

The man who entered the boardroom with him slides between the pair. He pushes Ethan away. "Back off."

"Who the hell are you?" Ethan yells.

"Ethan!" Jazz shouts, leaving the boardroom. "Stop. Leave them alone."

Ethan turns to Jazz and walks up to her. "Why won't you marry me? We'd be a great team and your father was on my side."

"Because I'm not a commodity for you to buy." She jabs his chest. "Stop trying to use me as a pawn in your little scheme."

Darius steps behind his daughter. "Ethan, my office. Go cool down. I'll be in in a minute."

Ethan rolls his eyes and turns toward the elevator. He keeps the corner of his eye on Darius and Jazz. Darius curls a finger under Jazz's chin, asking if she's sure this is what she wants. Jazz smiles sweetly, nodding. Darius whispers he is proud of her, and Ethan tries to not throw up in his mouth.

Home

Adrian takes Jazz's hands and clears his throat. "I can't apologise enough for what happened." He pauses and shifts his weight. "The locket. I'll find it, I promise. It'll take some time, but I'll track down the person who sold it for me and get information. I'm dedicated to finding it for you."

Jazz shakes her head, giving his hands a comforting squeeze. "It's ok. The important part will already be gone." Her eyes wet as she continues. "There was a lock of my mother's hair inside. She died when I was born, so it was the only part of her I had. That's what hurt so much. Everything else we could replace. You're right, people with money are wasteful with it."

His heart thuds. "I shouldn't have said any of that stuff."

"The locket has been gone for years. It was a shock when the wound reopened." Jazz tries for a smile and her olive skin glows. "I can honour my mother's memory. You've helped me heal in a whole new way."

"*Kiss her*," Gene whispers by their side. His fists sit under his chin in anticipation.

Adrian blushes and looks away, smiling. He feels Jazz's grip on his hands increase as her laughter plays like music.

"Will you take me back?" Jazz asks. "At the shelter. I'd really like to help."

Adrian looks back at the boardroom and around the hall. "You really wanna give all of this up?"

"These aren't my people."

Adrian's stomach twists. "I don't know if there will be anything to go back to. The shelter's bankrupt."

Jazz steps in closer and Adrian almost loses strength in his knees from the sweet, floral scent of her perfume. "That's where I come in. I'll back you."

He raises an eyebrow. "You mean money?"

"Let me be the financial backer and teach me how to work alongside you."

"You'd really do that?"

She smiles, captivating every part of Adrian. "I'd be honoured." She takes a step back, looking him up and down. "So is this going to be your new day-to-day attire?"

"Ah no," Adrian says, dropping her hands. "I let Genie work his magic, but I plan to go back to my t-shirt and jeans."

"I was happy to help," Gene says. "While I could, anyway. I guess I have to go back home? If I have a home to go back to, that is. I'm not exactly welcome there."

Adrian holds a breath and then smiles at the kid. "You're not going anywhere. We'll keep you around."

"What? Really?" Gene asks, ready to bounce.

"We can find you a job at the shelter, but you have to stay in school," Adrian says.

Gene leaps in the air and loops his arms around Adrian's neck. He glues his cheek against Adrian's, profusely repeating, "Thank you, thank you!"

"I'll ask Eddy to get the social workers to back off," Adrian says as Gene unravels from him.

"He could get emancipated," Jazz suggests. "I have a good lawyer."

"Emancipated?" Gene asks. "You know about that stuff?"

"I had a big fight with my dad when I was sixteen and had papers drawn up. He ended up giving me shares in the company to make amends, and I dropped it."

Adrian and Gene look at each other with mouths ajar.

"I know, I know," Jazz laughs. "Different worlds."

Worthy

"**Ethan**, it's not over," Darius says as Ethan paces in front of his desk. "Have patience, Son."

"Shut up with your patience," Ethan snaps, his muscles tensing with fury.

"I can't accept Jazz not being a part of Ultimate ME's future. You know that. We have to wait."

Ethan stops by the bar and pours himself a whisky. "Wait for what? You just announced her resignation."

"I don't believe she'd have such a wild change of heart," Darius says. "She will come back around. She always does. Then you two will battle head-to-head again."

"You want to keep me around so Jazz can prove herself worthy? How did *I* become the pawn in all of this?" He swigs the entire glass in one mouthful.

"She's going through a phase. She's always fought me on things, but she always ends up agreeing with me. In a perfect world, you two will work side-by-side."

"We need her to stay on for social media. We took a real hit the days she was absent. Engagement plummeted.”

“You should go to her and offer the position. Be civil and apologetic.”

Ethan groans and pours another whisky.

“Roth, put the glass down, or you’ll be the one I’ll be sending to rehab.”

Ethan rolls his eyes and sits the glass on the bar cart.

“I want you and Jazz moving the company forward, as a family. You will continue under my mentorship and you can lead Jazz like a big brother.”

Ethan walks to the leatherback armchair and flops down. “Big brother, hey? Whatever floats your boat.”

“Enough with the boats, Ethan.”

Win

Jazz wipes down a table in the dining room, the following week, and moves by Adrian's side. "You really are ok with me working here?"

Adrian wraps an arm around her and smiles. "Of course."

Awkward jitters take over them and they pull apart.

Jazz laughs and wipes her brow. "You know, I've never let myself fall for anyone before."

Adrian gulps. "Yeah?"

Jazz bites her lip and steps in close again. "With you, it's like you gave me no choice." She takes pleasure in his bashfulness. "Your infectious optimism, fierce loyalty, and pure honesty. How could I not fall for you?"

"I've never met a more stubborn, independent, kickass woman in all my life." Adrian grins, lacing his fingers with hers. "And I never would have imagined she liked me back."

Jazz leans into him and pushes her lips onto his. Their arms wrap around each other and the warmth from their kiss radiates throughout their bodies.

With giggles, they pull apart.

Jazz brushes back her hair and asks, "So what should I do next? I'm ready for more instructions."

Adrian's hand follows hers through her hair, and tingles sliver down her body.

"Never thought I'd hear those words," Adrian teases. "Jazz wants to wait and be shown what to do? She's not perfect?"

Jazz laughs and playfully hits his arm. "You know I'm trying to work on my patience and humility."

Adrian rubs his arm. "Careful, you're stronger than me, ya know."

Jazz wiggles her eyebrows. "Perhaps I can set up a fitness routine for you."

"Oh, like a trade-off, you think?" Adrian beckons her to follow him into the hall.

"Yeah, I'll whoop your butt," Jazz says as they make their way through the hall towards the common room.

"Anyone ever tell you you're too competitive?"

"No such thing."

They stop by the donation room to see Gene sorting the clothes into sizes and colours.

"Having fun?" Jazz asks.

Gene huffs. "Thank goodness I'm here. These clothes were screaming for help."

"Just make time to study," Adrian says, leaning against the doorframe. "Just because your classes are online doesn't mean you can slack off."

Gene *tsks*. "I'm not. Tessa has another job interview that she needs to get ready for." Gene gestures to Tessa, who shyly waves from behind a clothes rack. "I'm trying to find her an outfit in time."

"Sounds like you found him the perfect job," Jazz says cheerily.

"He's taking it a little too seriously." Adrian whispers with a cheeky smile.

"Tessa," Jazz says, "make sure you come find me at dinner, ok?

We will go over those interview questions to boost your confidence."

Tessa nods, her smile expanding. "Sure thing. Thanks, Jazz."

Jazz and Adrian move on towards the common room where Eddy walks out and into the hall.

"Ed, I was about to take on Jazz at pool," Adrian says, winking at Jazz. "If she doesn't take it too seriously. Wanna join us?"

"Thanks, but I'm heading to the swimming pool to get in some laps."

"That's becoming quite a regular habit," Jazz says.

Eddy nods, grinning. "I'll catch you guys later."

Jazz hurries into the common room. "Let's make teams." She looks at the boys on the couch. "I get Ferg."

Ferg stands up, throwing a fist in the air. "Because she knows I'm the best."

Adrian follows behind, clicking his fingers at Max. "Help me beat them."

Max rubs his hands together, making his way to the pool table. "Let's do this."

Jazz nudges Ferg. "We got this."

Adrian smiles across the table at her, and she melts inside. *Maybe throwing the game wouldn't be a bad idea. He could use a win.*

Jazz's story will continue in the following book...

Sneak Peek: Aria
Chapter One

Aria follows her family into St Paolo's Restaurant. It's one of the finest restaurants in the dining precinct between Province and the Business District. It has the traditional red and white checkerboard tablecloths, chunky white candle centrepieces, and the perpetual smell of pepperoni, meatballs, and parmesan cheese. It's a place that should be out of her parents' price range, but they deemed this celebration the most special of occasions.

Pride shimmers in her father's eyes as the hostess shows the family to their reserved table.

"Bottle of champagne," her father, Angelo, orders as they take their seats. "We are here to celebrate my daughter Aria's great achievement."

Aria smiles, glad to see her parents' happiness, yet she is very aware of her seething sister beside her. She can't decide which fear is greater. Not fulfilling her parents' wildest dreams or making her sister Valeria angry. And she didn't know how to do one without doing the other.

When champagne fills their glasses, Aria notices the tears welling in her mother's eyes. "You ok, Ma?" she asks.

Her mother smiles and nods. "Very."

"To Nationals!" Angelo cheers, raising his bubbling champagne glass.

All four glasses meet in the middle of the table.

Clink.

"Yes, Aria," Valeria says, after a sip of champagne. "You've got a lot of work ahead of you."

"As you should have," Angelo remarks.

Irritation drags Valeria's frown downward. Her eyes narrow and her glare intensifies at Aria.

Aria sets her champagne glass down and shifts on her seat. She clears her throat and then says, "I hope I don't disappoint you all."

"We'll work hard," Angelo says and takes another sip of champagne. "With my coaching, you will win the championship." His eyes move to Valeria. "We won't fail."

Valeria's jaw rocks, and when she moves on her seat, Aria flinches in reaction.

"Jumpy, Aria?" Valeria asks, mockingly.

Aria picks up a menu, but her trembling fingers betray her.

A whisper of laughter escapes her sister.

"Angelo Rivera!" a voice booms from the entrance of the restaurant.

The family turns to the voice and finds Angelo's brother and his family. Angelo's body tightens, and a scowl twists his expression.

"Long time no see," Aria's Uncle Franco says, stepping their way.

Aria looks past him to see her cousins, especially Helen. It has been years since they last saw one another. Aria gets a flash of the pair in the church choir robes they would wear every Sunday. She musters enough courage to wave at Helen.

"You can't find another restaurant to go to?" Angelo says with a clenched jaw.

Franco's arms shoot out wide. "We come here every Saturday

night. We never see you here. I assumed you couldn't afford it."

"I can afford more than you think," Angelo grumbles.

"Since when?" Franco asks with a jovial laugh. He crosses his arms and sends a smirk to his wife. "You still being a wimp, Angelo? Shutting your family away from the public?"

"No concern of yours," Angelo says, picking up a menu and shifting in his seat.

"Johnny and Lou will be here soon with their families," Franco says. "Please, come to your senses and re-join the family. This so-called feud is silly."

Angelo stands, throwing his napkin over his place-setting. "To you, maybe."

Aria's stomach cramps. She knows her father's actions well and doesn't like where this encounter is going.

"Don't be like this, Angelo," Franco says with a sour frown. "No one cares about how poor you are or how much time you waste by the edge of the swimming pool. You don't have to shut yourself off just because—"

"—Let's go," Angelo barks at his family. He lifts his arm up with force. "Up! Now!"

Aria, her mother and sister get up from their seats and promptly follow Angelo away from the table.

Franco's arms swing out wide and his mouth hangs open. "Please. Come on."

Angelo flicks a hand Franco's way, avoiding eye contact as he marches towards the restaurant's front door.

"You're being ridiculous," Franco calls out as the family exits onto the sidewalk.

Angelo grabs Aria's wrist, pulling her uncomfortably close. "You will win the Championship. Don't you dare make me look like a fool."

Aria's shoulders bunch high as she cowers beneath his heaving frame. "Yes, Pappa."

Angelo lets her go, tossing her arm with frustration.

"Nice going," Valeria snides, nudging Aria's arm as she brushes past.

Valeria's right eyebrow arches high as she follows her father to the car, keeping her stare on Aria. Enjoyment curls her lips.

Aria looks back to the restaurant. Helen gives her a defeated smile and a limp wave goodbye.

At home, Aria escapes into the shower. She turns the water as hot as it will go. Hot water is a rare nicety. She closes her eyes and the water cascades over her hair. Aria takes a half step back, so the water hits her face. For a moment, she holds her breath and takes in the sound of her heartbeat.

Slow and low.

Happiness is another rare nicety. When was the last time she felt that? She remembers it feeling similar to hot water, and that makes her smile. Seeing Helen reminds her of happiness. Reminds her of singing.

A hymn from church plays at her tongue, and she lets the melodic lyrics glide from her throat and echo in the shower. Her heart flutters at the freedom in making music with her voice and she opens her eyes.

The song stays in her head as she dresses and then disappears as she makes her way up the hall to her bedroom.

Aria sits at her dresser and glides her hairbrush through her damp auburn hair. She watches herself in the dresser mirror. Her strokes are gradual and gentle. Brushing her hair is the closest to peace she feels. A moment just for her.

Valeria bursts into their twin bedroom and pounces on her bed. "You really screwed up tonight, Aria."

Aria continues with her brush strokes, watching her sister from the corner of her eye. "Aren't you going to say your prayers before laying on your bed?"

Valeria groans and pulls herself off the bed.

Valeria kneels beside her bed, clasping her hands in front of her face. "Dear God, please watch over my family…" Aria tenses every time her sister tells her prayers aloud. It always sounds like prayers that God would look unkindly on. "…and especially look out for my little sister, Aria. She has so much work to do. So much pressure on her shoulders. Hopefully, the pressure doesn't hold her under water too long."

"*Valeria*," Aria whispers.

"Amen," Valeria says, and makes the sign of the cross. She flicks her eyes to Aria with a devious smile. "What? You know you shouldn't interrupt someone in the middle of prayer."

"You shouldn't say such mean-spirited things to God."

"It wasn't. I genuinely hope the pressure doesn't drown you."

Chills race down Aria's spine. Her jaw clenches and her trembling forces her to drop the hairbrush on the dresser.

"Say your prayers, dear sister," Valeria says, pulling back the covers on her bed.

Their bedroom is small and narrow. Their shared dresser and compact wardrobe crowd the space near the door. Their single beds fit snuggly against the walls with space for one person to kneel between them. The walls are cloud grey, and a picture frame hangs over each bed. An image depicting the Madonna hangs over Valeria's bed, and an image of Christ hangs over Aria's bed. A small window sits between the beds, and even though it's only working-class Hamlet outside, the view is the most interesting thing about the bedroom.

Aria moves to her bed and views pieces of broken scissors between the sheets of Valeria's bed. "Why do you have that in your bed?"

Valeria winks. "I'm making you a present."

Aria shivers as she turns her back on her sister and kneels by her bed. She makes the sign of the cross and clasps her hands. She takes in a deep breath and closes her eyes.

Dear God, is life supposed to be this hard? I'm eighteen. Am I supposed to decide things for myself now? Or do I have to wait until I'm married and out from under this roof?

Please, God, help Pappa. He is so mad. Is it because he's sad? His whole life is a fight with his brothers. If I

don't win Nationals, he'll never forgive me. Please, help me be strong. I need to win for him. And Mamma.

Please, watch over Valeria. She is mad too. She is mad at me. She blames me for beating her at the State Championships. She blames me for her not placing. Please, help her cope. I know she's a good person. There is a good person in my sister. She is just lost. I can help her. Please, show me how to help her.

Amen.

Aria opens her eyes and slides onto her bed.

"Did you ask God to take you in your sleep?" Valeria asks, twirling a jagged blade between her fingers.

Aria's body is so tense she might snap in half. "What?"

"You know," Valeria replies, reclining on her bed. "*If I die before I wake…*"

"Oh. No, I didn't say that prayer."

"But what happens when you die in your sleep?"

"When?"

"Everyone dies one day, dear sister."

"I'm tired," Aria says, flicking off the lamp between their beds. "Good night, Valeria."

Valeria snickers to herself. "Ok. Good night."

Aria pulls the covers to her chin. Darkness consumes the room, yet her eyes seem glued open. Her mind rewinds to her last choir practice. It was four years ago, but seeing Helen tonight makes the memory feel like yesterday.

Reminiscing is too painful.

Aria's jolts out of her thoughts by the sounds of a blade sharpening. She looks to her side and springs to sitting. The dark outline of her sister sits on her bed, clinking broken pieces of metal together.

"*Valeria*," Aria hisses, a hand resting on her terrorised heart.

"What? Were you sleeping?" Valeria asks with a hint of glee.

Aria's falls back to the mattress, confused by her sister's words.

With agility, Valeria launches off her bed, a blade directed at Aria.

Aria pushes towards the wall; a scream rushing out her.

Valeria shooshes her, running a blade delicately over Aria's cheek.

"Don't wake Ma and Pappa," Valeria warns in a whisper. "Then you'll really be in trouble."

Valeria moves back to her bed, flinging the piece of metal towards Aria's bed.

Aria squeaks in fright, flinging the ridged metal off her wrist. The serrated edge nicks her skin. The scratch is hot, and she puts pressure on the area. It oozes slightly, but not bad enough for a bandage.

Why is she always taking these things from Pa's tool shed? She collects these items and only does wicked things with them.

Aria lets out a weighted breath and looks to her sister's bed. A shadowy lump curls up on the bed.

She lies down, feeling more awake than ever. *Not the first night without sleep.* She eyes her sister's blanketed body and feels a new level of rigid. She will stay this tense until she hears sleep noises from Valeria. Even then, any sleep she gets will be broken by her self-inflicted nightmares.

THANK YOU FOR READING

To continue with the **Happily After When** Series, look out for the following books:

> #2 – <u>ARIA</u>
>
> #3 – <u>CARA</u>
>
> *And many more to come!*

Other books by Emily Bourne

The **In It Together** Series:

> #1 – <u>**In A Mirror**</u>
>
> #2 – <u>**In The Haze**</u>
>
> #3 – <u>**In It Together**</u>
>
> *And many more to come*

The **Holiday Together** Short Story Collection:

> #1 – <u>**In Fiji**</u>
>
> #2 – <u>**In Chills**</u>
>
> #3 – <u>**In The Spirit**</u>

CONNECT WITH THE AUTHOR

Visit author **Emily Bourne** in the following places:

Website
www.hcpbooks.com

Newsletter
www.freebies.hcpbooks.com

Instagram
www.instagram.com/iemilybourne

Facebook

www.facebook.com/authoremilybourne

Amazon

www.amazon.com/Emily-Bourne

BookBub

www.bookbub.com/authors/emily-bourne

GoodReads

www.goodreads.com/EmilyBourne

Join Emily Bourne's newsletter for a free ebook, writing and lifestyle updates, and some way-too-cute cat photo

www.ingramcontent.com/pod-product-compliance
Lightning Source LLC
Chambersburg PA
CBHW050852190726
48286CB00007B/2344